The Art of a Butterfly

Jo Priestley

The Women of Old Yorkshire Collection

First published in 2024

Copyright © Jo Priestley, 2024

All rights reserved. No part of this book may be used or reproduced in any form whatsoever without written permission except in the case of brief quotations in critical articles or reviews.

This book is a work of fiction. Names, characters, businesses, organisations, places, events and incidents either are the product of the author's imagination or are used fictitiously. Any resemblance to actual persons, living or dead, events, or locales is entirely coincidental.

For more information visit:

http://www.womenofoldyorkshire.com

ISBN 9798324608156

Other titles in the Women of Old Yorkshire collection:

The Calling of Highbrook
The Strangers in Me
Little Robin
Delfina – A Grown Up Fairytale
Orla Metcalfe Has Run Away
The Fifty Lost Christmases of Dolly Hunter

Acknowledgements

My late mum told me the love story of Constance and Lawrence who were born over a hundred years ago. Although I have changed their names and circumstances, at the heart of it all is the story of two people who alter drastically during their years together. It fascinated me as much as it did my mum when she used to visit them as a young girl.

Thoughts and feelings are my driving force when I write because they captivate and enthrall me. Their love story compelled me to write it.

Thank you to Andrew for editing my seventh book so patiently and supporting me and my work, and to Enrique Meseguer for the artwork on the book cover.

Thank you also to (in alphabetical order) Ann, Janet, Sue and Tracey, my regular reviewers who make me believe in my writing ability, encouraging me to keep going, which is so precious to me.

Chapter 1
1929—Lawrence Alexander Armitage

She skirts around the edge of my desk with surprising speed and stealth, coming to a standstill only inches away from me. She's breaching that invisible cord running down the centre which has served as a barrier to the uninvited for so long like the till side of a shop counter.

My breathing is loud, my eyes level with the knot at the end of her long string of pearls, the scent of her perfume overpowering rather than pleasant. I make to jump from my seat, my discomfort now insufferable but her hand bears down on my forearm with startling force. I shall not be able to leave this chair without a struggle. I've seen these very same hands perform her tasks with skill and dexterity for many years, always appearing feminine and harmless. Now, one of them has me pinned to my seat, leaving me wondering what could possibly have got into her this afternoon.

It began with the gift.

My eyes remained glued to the open box when she presented it to me, but the sensation of being studied, scrutinised even as she awaited my reaction made my heart race. Eighteen festive seasons have come and gone with a tie, a book, a bottle of wine at most, so why on Christmas Eve, 1929 would Daphne Farrington decide to buy me a set of gold, monogrammed cufflinks for my Christmas box? They are far too expensive, far too personal in fact. The ostentatious cufflinks would be suitable as a gift from perhaps a mother to her son on his twenty-first birthday or from a wife to her husband.

That gift was entirely inappropriate.

The tiny black velvet box in my hand was weighing heavier with each passing second. My mouth opened then closed, unsure how to respond without causing offence. I would never want to offend Daphne and I encouraged myself to believe that she had the best of intentions when she made her choice.

Earlier, as soon as the seven oak doors were locked and bolted to signal close of business, I made my rounds of the shop floor. I then distributed simple, but I hoped, valued gifts to the staff. The sound of the brass bolts sliding into their beds was ceremonious and you could almost hear each member of staff—me included—expunging a great sigh of relief that another frantic season had come to an end.

The signs are that it will be a new high in takings and this is in no small way down to the efforts and ideas of Daphne Farrington.

Lewis's Department Store will close for one whole day and reopen at ten o'clock on Boxing Day. The slightly later start will allow staff and customers alike a little longer to recover from the over-indulgence of the day before.

Gentlemen were presented with sandalwood soap, ladies with a small bottle of toilet water, neither too garish nor too frugal a gift. This year the toilet water was lavender-scented, but other scents have been proffered in previous years.

My wife, Constance, wrapped all one hundred and seventy-three parcels in red wrapping paper and finished them off with a dark green satin bow. Then over the course of a week I hand-wrote the gift tags with a personal note of thanks. I'm under no illusion that my staff are why I am where I am today. I have no doubt about it, and I take care to show how much I value each and every one of them from the bell boy to the floorwalkers. How festive the parcels looked in baskets on the landing when I left for work only this morning. They were ready and waiting to be collected by Timothy, my driver, who discreetly delivered them to Daphne at the back entrance to the store. All very surreptitious and fun.

Of course, before I married it was Daphne who was tasked with wrapping the presents for her colleagues, but Constance insisted she was only too happy to take over the duty from her.

"I'm sure Ms Farrington has plenty on her plate, especially in a busy department store this time of year. It would give me great pleasure to organise the staff gifts, Lawrie," she told me in the October of our first year of marriage.

Was it over nine years ago already?

So, it was agreed. Daphne said it was a very thoughtful gesture from Constance who has been doing the same every year since.

Now the end of my day has been somewhat foiled, and all because of an ill-chosen gift.

"Ms Farrington, I am very grateful to you for such a thoughtful gift, truly I am," I said to her, "but I can't possibly accept the cufflinks. They are far too … generous."

I was satisfied with my choice of word as I swung from side to side on the brass casters of my office chair. The leather was making me overheat in my suit jacket, but I was finding it impossible to sit still.

Her smile, at first beaming and then thin, slipped from her face and she patted her perfect dark hair at the nape of her neck. I've never seen her with a hair out of place in all the years I've known her. She travels on the tram to work in all weathers but always arrives looking elegantly coiffed with her fashionable chin-length hairstyle.

"Then I wonder who else can make use of the cufflinks. I doubt it will surprise you to know that there are no other gentlemen I'm acquainted with who have the initials *L.A.A.*"

A slightly nervous titter escaped her. My assistant is not a jovial person by any stretch of the imagination, so it was all rather awkward. Perhaps the best plan of action, I thought then, is to receive the cufflinks with good grace and simply hide them in a drawer for the time being.

"Indeed, I see your point," I said, hoping my smile was warm. "Well then, I thank you sincerely for your considerate gift, Ms Farrington."

I placed the box next to the fountain pen on my desk, carefully aligning it alongside and patting it in the hope of convincing her how delighted I was with it.

My expectation then was for her to wish me a merry Christmas before donning her coat and hat, ready to leave *Lewis's* to commence her quiet celebrations.

Instead, she remains far too close for comfort still, though thankfully she has at least removed her hand from my forearm.

"Mr Armitage, please forgive me, I know this is highly irregular," she says now. "However, I must ... I must speak with you. The Christmas break is upon us, and I simply cannot wait a moment longer. The alternative would be far worse."

Her chest is heaving, her eyes sparkling with tears. For the first time, her face is close enough for me to notice her eyes are green, filtering outwards from the pupil to a shade of taupe like leaves in the midst of shedding their summer hue. I have no idea why they should remind me of such. Her cheeks and neck down to the collar of her starched, white blouse have turned a glowing shade of pink. This uncharacteristic bordering on hysterical behaviour is disconcerting to the point of making me almost lightheaded. Up until this moment, I have always known her to be the embodiment of professionalism, so she has suddenly become a stranger.

Only moments ago, in the quiet excitement of my mind, I was heading out of the deserted store to drive home in the snow with Timothy so I could enjoy the Christmas break with Constance and our daughter, Dora. Now it appears our celebrations are to be delayed.

"I must say it," she says, "I cannot spend another Christmas Day with mother and George, maintaining the pretence." When she pauses, I can see she is teetering on the precipice of her next words, debating whether to jump into that abyss. I draw a huge intake of breath, willing her to call a halt to whatever proclamation she is about to make.

"I confess I shall be thinking only of you the whole day, and … and I just can't sit through the impossible charade for yet another year … and I shan't, I tell you."

She buries her head in her hands, weeping suddenly like a small child who has unburdened themselves of a terrible secret, all the while knowing it will get them into trouble.

I would never have expected Daphne Farrington to lose her composure in such a dramatic fashion. I try to quash the uneasy thought that there can be no going back from this conversation; this is not a harmless childish secret which will be salved with a few words of comfort.

Blowing out my cheeks I get to my feet to place a hand on her shoulder. I feel her trembling under my palm and have a flood of compassion. Despite the nature of her confession, I only wish to relay my sympathies exactly as I would do with any person in distress.

However, my stomach twists when I realise this is not just any person; Daphne has been my loyal assistant, my rock both here and in my previous position in Bradford for some eighteen years.

"Come, sit by the fire," I say, my voice little more than a whisper. "Let me pour us a stiff drink to settle our nerves."

When she doesn't make a move, I place a hand gently between her shoulder blades to guide her to the fireside chair. I'm about to offer her my handkerchief when she produces a crisp one of her own from her dress pocket.

The drink's cabinet sits beside a floor to ceiling bookcase displaying an impressive collection of classics that I know I will never again find the time to read.

The tabletop becomes hazy now as I absorb the enormity of her outburst. Daphne Farrington has just declared she has romantic feelings for me. Worse still, it appears these feelings have been buried for such a long time they have become deep-rooted enough to put us both in this lamentable position.

Whisky and brandy sit shoulder to shoulder in sparkling crystal decanters. I make a snap decision that brandy might be the better option, though hardly fitting to offer a lady. Sherry or port would be preferable, but it's the first and I sincerely hope the last time a lady will be weeping in my office.

There's a strange irony in that Daphne is usually the person to handle any delicate matters of the heart involving female members of staff. She has been my trusted shield from such things until today.

I pour two small brandies into large balloon glasses, gulping one of them down before quickly refilling the glass. Rejoining Daphne, I offer her the other glass, ensuring I keep my eyes on the amber liquid flickering like a candle in the firelight. Our fingers touch briefly, and I snatch my hand away in the hope of pretending it never happened.

It only serves to have the opposite effect.

These wing chairs have, until now, been reserved for business conversations. They have seen many a deal sealed with investors and suppliers alike and many a strong connection has been formed. Some have become much more than a professional alliance—Gregory Coleman springs immediately to mind.

This Christmas Eve however, there is no lively business banter taking place, instead I am sitting and suffocating in oppressive silence. Daphne must be the one to continue the conversation, as I would only be a fool to assume anything from her brief statement. Her woeful expression is unnerving, forcing me to turn my eyes to the fire.

"I know this is far from what you will have been expecting to happen this afternoon, Mr Armitage," she says, her words partly muffled by her handkerchief. "If it's any consolation, I'm as thrown by this turn of events as you will be. I know little of it, but perhaps we are pushed to breaking point at the most inconvenient of times because our emotions are heightened by outside influences. In this case, I assume it to be Christmas."

I imagine she has little experience of heightened emotion. I've certainly never seen any sign of it and now I have a front row seat to witness the poor woman's unravelling. The end of her nose is chafed, her hair slightly ruffled on one side, on the other her usual flawless waves.

I have been gripping my brandy glass so tightly I realise it has been at risk of shattering in my hand.

"I see," I say flatly, then wonder how to take control of the conversation. She sits tweaking the lace of her handkerchief on her lap with her thumb. "I only know I cannot let you leave in such a distressed state of mind. I have a duty of care towards all my staff."

My tone is benign, non-committal but I hope not unfriendly. She leans her head backwards to fall on the indent of the leather on the chair back. Her eyes are raised to the ceiling.

My assistant has often been the topic of conversation with members of the Board. Comments about her unflappable manner, her beauty, and how she would make someone a wonderful wife have always flowed thick and fast when she leaves the room. I dismiss them with a nod and a polite smile, as I've heard the same mutterings for many a year.

"Mr Armitage, I mustn't continue to mislead George, Mr Jackson, about my intentions. It is cruel when all I can think about is someone else." Her eyes are still fixed on the ceiling. "Surely, you must have sensed something over the years."

I stop myself just in time from declaring emphatically that I most certainly have not suspected anything whatsoever.

Her right foot taps manically on the fireside rug.

"I think you are mistaken, Ms Farrington, I have never suspected you had anything other than the warmest *professional* regard towards me. We have worked together for a long time, but, out of the office, we know so little of each other."

Her throat is fluttering, and I pray she won't start to weep again. I'm reeling from her declaration and concerned for her welfare yet no good can come from this disturbing conversation.

Time is running out for me to play with Dora before Mrs Osmond, the housekeeper, puts her to bed. She will be giddy with excitement for tomorrow, like all six-year-old children should be and we will be infected by it. Afterwards Constance and I will place Dora's presents under the tree and sit by the fire with a sherry before supper. Then just before retiring ourselves, we will pop into our daughter's bedroom to hang a stocking on the end of her bed to greet her in the early hours of Christmas Day morning. She will run into our room with the stocking dangling from her hand, climbing onto our bed for us to watch her pull out a shiny sixpence, an apple, an orange, and some small token Constance will have chosen as a gift for her.

Now instead of going home I must sit here and face an uncomfortable truth.

"Forgive me, but I'm finding it difficult to understand. I know at least that you're aware I'm married, and I have been for some ten years."

Her head rises from the chair back to face me, her eyes clashing with mine for the first time.

"Obviously I know you are married…" she stops talking, her face now taut as granite and I grow increasingly hot under her gaze. How could I have misled her; does she see my lack of mention of my family as a sign they are not important to me? Smoothing her wayward hair behind her ears, she dabs her nose and I see signs of Ms Daphne Farrington returning.

"I see I have made a terrible fool of myself," she mutters, almost to herself.

She pushes herself up with the chair arms to check her appearance in the oval mirror hung above the mantle. Wiping her eyes with her crumpled handkerchief she straightens her collar before setting down her shoulders, as though standing to attention on parade.

I also feel terrible, the guilt making the acid in my stomach curdle my luncheon. I must quickly think of something to say to soothe her. I get up from my chair to stand by her side.

"You are a very attractive woman, Ms Farrington, please do not think for one moment that I'm not flattered by your confession today."

The words sound hollow and insincere even to me, only a cliché.

A funny little laugh escapes her, one so soft I could barely hear it even in the hush of the room.

"I wonder, Mr Armitage, did no-one tell you that, 'I'm flattered but…' is possibly the most crushing rebuff a person could ever receive?"

Until this moment, I had no idea. I only thought it the best way to let someone down as gently as possible. Now I feel a heel for using the phrase in the past.

"I can only apologise," I say, inclining my head slightly. "I thought I might only upset you further if I was too frank."

Perhaps now is precisely the time to be frank, I think. There was clearly a moment when she saw something, be it a glance or a gesture which was the making of her own imagination.

"It appears I have given you the wrong impression by keeping my work and home life separate. The truth is, although I rarely talk about my wife at work, I have always loved her … and it might be better to say now, to avoid any future misunderstanding, that I always will."

We study each other's reflection in the mantle mirror, colour rising in my cheeks from speaking in such a manner. Her green eyes narrow slightly, her lips settling in a hard line, but I must not look away or my words will be diminished.

"You know, sir, I have always considered *always* to be a very long time," she says, her face now breaking into a bright smile. "Well then, I think all that is left for me to do is to extend my warmest greetings of the season to you and to your family."

We have yet to break eye contact though my willpower is beginning to fail me.

"Thank you, Ms Farrington," I say, only too relieved now to respond in our familiar way. "I too extend the same greeting to you and indeed to your mother."

The binding of our eyes is finally severed as she swiftly turns and exits the room. The catch on the door closes quietly behind her and silence returns.

My heart rate slows as I try to snuff out the memory of what has just happened in only a few moments. Daphne Farrington and I have never had a moment of unrest in all our years of working together.

Already doubts are creeping in about how I tackled the unforeseen events and what I might have done differently. Perhaps I was too honest; I have hurt her feelings when this was never my intention.

A trailing breath escapes me, recalling the disingenuous smile which did not pair with the cheery festive greeting she extended to me and my loved ones.

The blood in my veins suddenly runs ice cold, so I swig down the last of my brandy in one devouring gulp.

It does nothing to warm me.

Chapter 2
1919—Constance Crawford

"Mmm, it does indeed appear to be getting bigger," Dr Fitzpatrick says, circling a forefinger around my scalp.

I recoil from the feel of his hand on the smooth patch of skin I had hoped was barely noticeable. Even my own fingers dare not touch the patch which sits just below my crown and is currently around the size of a five-shilling coin. Not so long ago it was the size of a ha'penny; this is the way I've taken to measuring it and given the cost of seeing a doctor, it seems entirely appropriate.

I had no desire to come but mother insisted. It's now a fortnight since my first visit but the problem is clearly worsening. I'd been hiding the patch well until an ill-timed gust of wind blew my hair out of place when I was entering the house. It was a momentary lapse but as I turned to push the door against the gust, my ever-watchful mother saw what I had taken great pains to hide.

"Have you changed your eating habits in any way, Miss Crawford?" Dr Fitzpatrick asks now, returning to his desk to make more hastily scribbled notes. "Poor nutrition is known to be a factor in hair loss."

Mother shuffles in her seat and I already know what she is about to say before she says it.

"Doctor, I assure you my daughter is well-fed and nourished, I make certain of it."

Dr Fitzpatrick leans to pat mother's hand, which is tightly clenched on top of the handbag resting on her knee. She will be bristling from the doctor's unintended inference. She prides herself on nourishing and taking good care of me, ensuring she cooks two hearty meals a day for us, three on a weekend.

"Of course, forgive my careless choice of words," he says, his eyes darting between us, "but you know, young women can do these things on the quiet, Mrs Crawford."

Both their faces turn in unison towards me. I busy myself placing my hat back where it belongs, only too glad hide the evidence.

"Have you been up to something, Constance?" Mother asks.

Her face powder sits in the creases of her forehead as she raises her eyebrows. Her silver hair peeps above each ear from under a navy-blue felt halt. This one is currently her best hat as she always says that one must always look one's best when stepping outside of the house. This has been instilled in me all my life and every hat must match my coat, shoes and handbag each season.

"No, mother, of course not, I've eaten all your food and enjoyed it like always. I can't imagine what's happening to my hair, there must be another explanation."

Dr Fitzpatrick is scribbling away as we speak making me wonder if he's making a note about me or my mother's attitude.

"At this rate she'll have no hair by the autumn," she almost wails. "Is there nothing at all you can do doctor? Constance is such a beautiful girl, it would be terrible, simply terrible if she lost her lovely blonde curls."

The doctor holds his hand up to try to halt the torrent.

"I think perhaps you're jumping the gun, Mrs Crawford, one bald spot does not mean she will lose all her hair. I'll prescribe a hair tonic to use for a month and I'm certain by then Constance will see signs of improvement."

Mother sighs, her shoulders slumping slightly as she finally gets a hold on her emotions. She's staring at my hat, but I know she will still be dwelling on what is happening underneath. Over the weeks she has become obsessed with checking the size of it, and I imagine this will only grow worse until the problem is resolved. Surely, if anyone is going to go to pieces it should be me.

Dr Fitzpatrick hands mother a prescription and she folds it once before placing it in her handbag and snapping the catch shut.

"You can get the tonic from *Inghams*," he says with a comforting smile.

We say our farewells and I glance at Dr Fitzpatrick as we leave. He has removed his glasses, rubbing his eyes with a thumb and forefinger. I'm sure he's as exhausted as he looks because the gossip mongers informed us that he was up the whole night delivering Elsie Carr's daughter, her fifth and final, to hear her talk of late. She's been telling anyone who would listen for months that boy or girl, she's had enough children and that her Roy can take a running jump into the river if he wants them to try for a baby boy yet again.

The doctor drops his hand and glances at mother who is on her way out of the door.

"Constance," he whispers, "I didn't want to bring it up in front of your mother, but it was an awful thing that happened. It may be contributing to your condition, and I encourage you to make an appointment to see me at the surgery alone."

I'm caught fast, somewhere between panic and distress, my eyes stinging at the memory the doctor has now laid bare in front of me to address.

"Just think about it, that's all I ask," he says.

Nodding, I hurry from the room, swallowing uncontrollably to stop my tears.

"Come along, Constance," mother says now, glancing over her shoulder.

I know Dr Fitzpatrick is well-meaning, but I shall not be making the appointment. It would serve no purpose and it will not change the course of history.

We step out onto the shady side of the street. Even so the heat seeps through my cotton jacket to cling to my dress. Mother bustles ahead of me to the chemists which is located only a short distance away, and the door is held open for her.

The polite gentleman holding the door is very smartly dressed, his suit tailored to fit him perfectly and the hat in his hand of fine quality. Holding the door handle with his free hand, he waits for us to cross the threshold in turn, inclining his head slightly.

My, but he's handsome, I think, as my eyes flutter fleetingly to his face. The realisation makes me look away quickly, mumbling my thanks.

There are a few people waiting in line for their prescription to be administered, but it's nowhere near as busy as wintertime. I'm acutely aware of the gentleman's presence behind me as mother offers my prescription to Mr Ingham, the chemist. I've known Mr Ingham my whole life and as mother says, what he doesn't know about the population of Hunslet isn't worth knowing, such is the nature of his job.

"Good morning, Mrs Crawford; Constance," he says now, searching the counter until he finds his glasses.

We return his greeting, and he replaces them on the end of his nose to peer at the doctor's scrawl. As I watch him my heart beats a little faster, picking up speed until it's racing like a train. I recall suddenly how he tends to reiterate full instructions to customers on the correct dosage and usage of prescribed medication. He speaks in his best stage whisper but it's generally loud enough for anyone in the vicinity to overhear.

We stand to one side to wait when he disappears into the back room. If only I could remove my jacket without drawing attention to myself. The heat is cooking me through the huge glass window.

"Ah, a new face in town I see," Mr Ingham says on return taking the gentleman's prescription from him. "Welcome, sir, a pleasure to make your acquaintance."

"Thank you, and likewise," the gentleman says before rejoining the queue behind me. He catches my eye as he wafts past me with a small smile. My face is tight, and nerves are preventing me from returning his smile though I should like to. A twinkle in his eye makes him appear warm and kindly but even this will not unhinge my jaw.

My blouse is clinging to my back, and I search for mother who is now browsing the shelves. Mr Ingham will return any moment and I briefly consider fleeing the chemists before an alternative course of action springs to mind.

So, I bend my legs at the knees before crumpling elegantly to the floor. Mother's expression of alarm tweaks my guilty conscience before I quickly close my eyes to it. A commotion in the chemist will soon be forgotten, and it's a small price to pay.

I should hate to be humiliated in front of a man whose devastating looks would put any woman whomsoever at a distinct disadvantage.

Chapter 3
1919—Daphne Farrington

"Ah, here we are. Were your ears burning, Ms Farrington? I was just saying how you keep us all in line here and how grateful I am for it."

Surprise forces me to take a small step backwards. Thankfully, I'm able to recover quickly and stride with my hand outstretched towards the young girl in Lawrence's office. I went downstairs to fetch my lunch from the canteen only to return to see a stranger in our midst. It's perfectly obvious this is not a business associate.

"Daphne Farrington, how do you do?" I say, shaking her tiny limp hand. Man or woman, I much prefer a strong handshake, but I doubt this young lady has had many opportunities to shake hands with anyone.

"How do you do, Ms Farrington? I'm Constance Crawford," she says. "Mr Armitage has nothing but praise for your aptitude and your work."

How timid her voice is, breathy even. She's a pretty little thing, somewhat younger than Lawrie and not someone I would have expected to catch his eye, but he's watching over her with a proud smile.

"I thought I'd bring Miss Crawford to see where it all happens," he chuckles, making him suddenly appear younger. "But then I thought I would take the opportunity to share our good news with you."

It can't be, I think. Hope flows into then out of my consciousness as quickly as a bolt of lightning could strike me down.

He's getting married, I know it; the day has finally dawned.

I tripped down to the canteen only ten minutes ago to see what delights were on offer today, and now my sandwich shall sit uneaten on my desk. I can't imagine food ever being a concern of mine again.

All hope for my future has been culled in a breath.

I must cling to my composure. I secure a tight-lipped smile in place and look between them both with what I pray is an expression of expectancy.

They are oblivious as they smile at one another conspiratorially, glowing with the secret they still believe is theirs and theirs alone. They have no idea I am ahead of them, that I've sought to stay one step ahead of Lawrie since the first day we met.

My throat knots so tightly I'm struggling for air, so I must rest my hand lightly on the chair back. It's the same chair I sit in each weekday to take notes and instructions from the man I have worked with for six years.

"We are to be married, Ms Farrington," he says. "I've been waiting for the right moment to tell you and now it has presented itself."

Perhaps there could be a right moment for you, Lawrie, but never for me, I think. I widen my smile further so I must look like a sad clown. Still, they fail to notice because they now live in their own little world.

"Such wonderful news, congratulations!" I exclaim, the words booming and high-pitched.

"Thank you so much for your good wishes," the girl says, beaming his way. They exchange affectionate words without speaking, so I must watch on like a wretched third wheel.

"Thank you, Ms Farrington. I wasn't sure if Constance would have me, but then life is full of surprises," he says, with yet another quiet chuckle. "Her mother is still browsing downstairs, so I thought I might whisk her daughter up here to see my office."

I wander to one of the three tall windows and stare at the street scene below. They both join me, Lawrie at my shoulder, commenting on the outlook he can peruse on a whim each workday. I often catch him staring from the windows, deep in thought. Perhaps I should have seized the moment once to voice my affection for him.

Now though, I am too late.

The miniature shoppers are going about their lives, the toy-sized motorcars crawling the warren of roads as I think how right Lawrie is.

Life is indeed full of surprises.

*

Unlike so many men after the war, Lawrie came back full of zest and ready to build a successful career. It was as though he was making up for lost time. I was only too happy to help him on his way, and day by day he became my life's work.

Settling down never appeared to be on his agenda. The odd rumour surfaced from time to time about him seeing this girl or that, but then nobody materialised. Not until today.

His freedom and his breeding catapulted him to success. I know, and I'm certain others do, how exceptional he is with that rare combination of looks, intelligence, charm, money, but above all, a kind heart.

When he became the deputy manager at *Brigshaw & Muffs* in Bradford I set about making myself indispensable as his secretary because I suspected he wouldn't stay put for long. The day he left to manage *Lewis's* was dreadful, but I consoled myself that I only needed to bide my time. My wish came true a few months later when his new secretary became pregnant. It was no surprise when I received the telephone call from Lawrie explaining that I was the first person he thought of.

"Of course, you will have many more duties than a secretary, Ms Farrington," he said. "I'm thinking more of an assistant type of role. There will be many functions to attend, and I hope on occasion that you might accompany me. It's all part of the grand plan," he laughed down the telephone. "Hobnobbing with the shareholders goes with the job in this influential city and, as you know, I highly value your business acumen." He paused, and I was careful not to fill the silence. "Will you join me here if your mother will agree to move from Bradford?"

I do pride myself in keeping abreast of stocks and shares, of finance matters in general, and I was well aware he used this knowledge to his advantage. I see us as a team and to his credit, he does too. In that moment, it felt far more than a business proposal.

Mother will be fine, I thought then. Her life is small. No, it was someone else who was troubling me throughout the conversation, someone who has been waiting patiently in the wings for years: George Jackson. George is a good man, some might say he would make me the perfect husband, but he has one disadvantage I'm unable to see past, and one he can never alter:

He is not Lawrence Alexander Armitage.

The two men are incomparable. Lawrie is ambitious, while George is devoted only to me; Lawrie is gregarious and outgoing while George is quiet and shirks the limelight; Lawrie is strong but kind, while George is just … kind. 'Kindly, like your father,' is how my mother refers to him, not helping his case at all.

They do have one thing in common, however, in that they are decent, honest, trustworthy men who just so happen to be blessed with the heart-stopping good looks. Lawrie is dark, George fair, but nobody would fail to notice them when they walk by.

George came into my life about a year before Lawrie. I met him in a pub and I can't help but note that even how we met is a dull story. No clashing of eyes across a crowded room, no rescuing me from the path of an oncoming vehicle, only George asking me if I'd like another gin and tonic. I would be lying however if I said I wasn't taken by him, and throughout that first year we discussed getting married, having children much the same as every other couple. At the time I meant it too; those things had always been scattered on the unspoken path intended for my life, and I was content to meander down it with George for a while.

Then came the day Lawrie appeared at my desk to report for an interview for the deputy role at *Brigshaw & Muffs*. Confident without being overbearing, his smile made me glow like a bashful young girl. One businesslike introduction was all it took for me to know, like how I imagine one feels finding the perfect home or the perfect wedding dress that just suits to a tee and you need look no further.

My search was over.

Many a time, mother had told me her tale of falling in love with father the moment she saw him in his Royal Engineers uniform. She lived happily as an army wife until the day he died. But I was level-headed, sensible Daphne Farrington, head girl at my last school, pencil and milk monitor at my previous schools before then.

Daphne Farrington was far too pragmatic to be affected in such a way.

"That man will have my job if I'm not careful," Mr Williams, the manager, said when Lawrie left us after the interview. "The question is will it be in my best interests to employ him or should I persuade the Board that the second-choice candidate might be the better option?"

The lie tripped lightly from my tongue.

"Oh, I don't think you need to worry, Mr Williams," I simpered. "Everyone knows what an excellent job you're doing. In any case, if you go ... I go."

One eyebrow shot up his forehead, his lascivious grin making my stomach roll.

"You are a dark horse, Ms Farrington," he said. "I had no idea you felt so passionately."

I rued the lie as I then had to spend the next few years keeping the man at arm's length, whilst keeping him onside. All this I did gladly in the hope Lawrie might notice me in more than a professional capacity.

That was until The Great War came.

In 1914 Lawrie was among the first to volunteer and off he went to France with his pals without a second thought. It would surely not have been more of a wrench if he was my husband who had left me to fight for king and country.

Ever attentive, George noticed the change in me. I was pining for a man who wasn't mine and it was like a physical pain akin to homesickness and impossible to hide. He assumed I was anxious about the terrible conflict, which was, of course, completely plausible.

"When will you sign up?" I asked him one night on the way home from visiting his parents.

He and his father had discussed the war at length the whole afternoon, but to my mind, George had no right to an opinion when he was fighting the war from his armchair. I smiled sweetly at his mother when she rolled her eyes in mischief, but my food was sticking in my craw. Relief made me jump up too quickly when George said it was time to make a move.

He dropped his arm from around my shoulders, looking down at me like he had never considered the question before.

"They're saying it will be all over by Christmas," he said. "So, I really don't see the point in deliberately scuppering our future plans."

It was the wrong thing to say in the wrong moment, and it was there, hanging between us like a horrible smell. He left me with no alternative but to tackle it head on.

"Well, all I can say, George, is that it's a bloody good job the men already out there fighting aren't of the same mind as you."

His head hung as we walked in silence all the way home and when he dropped me at the door he didn't come in as usual. I raced straight up the stairs without even saying goodnight to my mother and threw myself on the bed, weeping for Lawrie whom I hadn't heard a whisper about for months. I was painfully aware I would be the last to hear any news when I was nothing but a lowly secretary.

Two days after our tense conversation, George joined the queue of men outside St George's Hall. The cheerful bravado of August was by then replaced with hollow, haunted looks and the knowledge that many would not return.

For the next three and a half years, I pined for Lawrie whilst feeling guilt-stricken about forcing George to fight. He would eventually have been called up anyway, but I couldn't shake the belief that if he was killed, his mother would lose her son and the blame would lie at my door. I lost over two stones in weight, becoming a ghostly wisp walking the moors around Haworth on a weekend to keep from under my mother's fretful eye.

She told me after the war that she realised then just how deep my love for George had grown. How wrong she was, but it kept her from the ugly truth.

Neither man died in the end, though Lawrie has an injury to his left shoulder that requires the use of opiates from time to time.

They were the lucky ones, and I should have been nothing but grateful for them to be home.

For the safe return of both men.

Chapter 4
1919—Constance

"Are you sure you're quite alright, dear?" mother asks for the third time.

I'm barely listening, only wondering how I can free myself from the purgatory of our parlour without appearing rude.

"Yes, please don't concern yourself, mother," I say. "It was only the excessive heat that made me faint."

The handsome gentleman now has a name: Mr Lawrence Armitage, though he is known to his friends as Lawrie. He is sitting at our table under the open window, watching me as intently as if I were a laboratory specimen. His jacket sits on the back of the chair, his tie only slightly loosened after requesting the privilege due to the stifling weather.

Mr Armitage, Lawrie, may be handsome, but he is indeed a gentleman. I know this already from the furrow of his brow as I opened my eyes to find him crouching by my side, and from the tender touch of his hand on my back as he helped me onto a stool in the back room of the chemist. I sipped the tumbler of water Mr Ingham presented me with, planting my eyes firmly on the floor.

"Might I enquire where you live, madam?" Lawrie asked mother who was leaning against a shelf of glass bottles, her face flushed and a slick of perspiration on her top lip.

"Only a few streets away and ordinarily we would walk on such a fine day, but under the circumstances, we will take the tram home today."

Mother thinks the price of a tram fare is an unnecessary expense we can ill afford, so she must have been worried about me. I know the people of Hunslet think we're far better off than we are, but she is very frugal with our household expenses. She stretches my late father's pension and my wage to surprising lengths and would nip a currant in two if it saved money, as my friend, Jennifer, from school says jokingly.

Lawrie insisted on escorting mother and I home safely, ignoring our pleas that we would be perfectly fine. At his insistence, I held his forearm to board the tram, and he paid our fares before sitting behind us for the duration of the admittedly short journey. After we alighted, he extended his arm once more, so I was sandwiched between him and mother for the seemingly endless walk along the two streets to Plevna Terrace.

And all I could think about during the tortuous journey home was the desperate lengths I was prepared to stoop in order to avoid my need of a hair tonic being disclosed.

"May I offer you more tea, Mr Armitage?" Mother asks now.

"No, but thank you, I'm thoroughly refreshed," he says with a bright smile.

His face turns my way and this time I manage to curve my lips slightly. Our eyes hold for a little longer

34

than expected, making my face burn, so now I am forced to look away.

"I hope you're feeling better now, Miss Crawford, you gave us quite a fright."

"Much better, thank you," I say, wondering how I can elaborate to avoid an awkward silence.

Thankfully, mother distracts us by opening the window wider to let in more fresh air. The noise increases from the children playing in the street and the neighbours are chattering now they have finished their morning chores.

"Where do you live, Mr Armitage?" Mother asks as she sits back down by my side on our small settee.

"I'm lodging with a friend at present. We went to university together and now I've come to manage the *Lewis's* store on the Headrow. I'm certain you will know it."

Mother opens her eyes and mouth wide as though she's discovered Lawrie is a distant cousin of the king. He may as well be in her mind as *Lewis's* is the place where she dreams of shopping. She used to take me at Christmastime to see Father Christmas and always bought a small gift for father. She must have saved all year to afford it. We still make our annual pilgrimage there as part of our build-up to the festivities.

"The manager, you say!" She exclaims, mightily impressed by our visitor.

Lawrie's laugh is low as he nods, clearly amused by her reaction.

"Yes, I've been there only a few months. I fully intend to rent a house when I actually find the time to look properly, but I would prefer not to rush the decision. I intend to stay in the area for the foreseeable future, at least. My roaming days are over."

I'm sure mother will be joining the dots as well as I am. This gentleman is clearly an eligible bachelor looking to settle down. There must surely be a young lady, because he is far too attractive to be alone *and* available.

"Yes, these things must not be rushed," mother says, the workings of her mind clear to me at least as to how she might uncover more details. Please be careful, mother, I think, I would hate to scare our visitor away. "Well, as they say, all work and no play make Jack a dull boy," she says with a knowing smile.

Lawrie appears unphased by her clumsy remark.

"Indeed, and I intend to make more time to play in the future."

Although his eyes are on mother, I know this is a secret code directed at me to decipher. I have no experience of flirtation, but somehow, I think I may just have encountered my first taste of it.

Still basking in the glow of our secret, I jump at the rat-tat-tat of the front doorknocker. Mother and I exchange glances, wondering who could be at the door as we never have unannounced guests. Not since she told Mrs Baxter next door that she had too much to be getting on with to sit around all day nattering. Mrs Baxter took the hint and never graced us with her presence again.

Mother opens the front door but from where we sit, Lawrie and I are unable to see who the caller is.

"Hello, Mrs Crawford," a familiar voice says cheerily. I gulp some air, a hand instinctively going to my throat and Lawrie looks alarmed at my reaction. "Sorry to bother you, but in all the kerfuffle we forgot to give Miss Crawford her prescription."

Young Tommy has been tasked with delivering medicine by Mr Ingham to the older and frailer residents of Hunslet. He's a regular feature, weaving the streets on his bicycle every day.

Please Tommy, just give mother the brown paper bag and be gone, I think, my heart pounding in my ears.

"Ah, yes, thank you, Tommy, I'll pass it on," mother says. "Miss Crawford is feeling much better now. Please relay my thanks to Mr Ingham, if you will be so kind."

She makes to close the door, offering Lawrie a little smile over her shoulder to ease the silence between us as we wait. There will be no chance of me thinking of anything to say to bridge it.

"I will, Mrs Crawford, but Mr Ingham said to tell you that Miss Crawford must rub the tonic on all her hair and not just the bald spot. There's more chance of saving the other hair then. Will you tell her for me?"

A quell of nausea almost overwhelms me as mother closes the door with a slight slam. She looks my way, all colour drained from her face.

The silence drags to the point where I think I may be sick. Oh, the shame of this moment will surely end any slim hope I might have had of meeting Lawrie again.

He jumps to his feet suddenly, and my eyes fix firmly on the rug. Clearly, he can't get out of our house quick enough.

"Well, Mrs Crawford, I thank you for your hospitality. You have been most kind and I'm glad you're feeling better, Miss Crawford. I must be on my way to work now, or my assistant will be wondering where I am. I only told her I would be in a little later this morning."

He's going into far too much detail, already with one foot out of the door in his mind, no doubt. He grabs his hat from the table, covering his dark waves with it, but this little scene unfolds in my peripheral vision as I shall never be able to look at the man again.

"Of course, I understand, Mr Armitage," mother says flatly, all previous excitement stripped from her voice. "Thank you for all you have done for us this morning, you went above and beyond your call of duty."

My heart almost stops now as one of his black brogues, shined to army perfection, takes a step closer to me.

"I wonder, Miss Crawford, if you would mind if I called on Sunday afternoon to ensure you are fully recovered. Perhaps if your mother was in agreement me might take a stroll around the area, that is if you could spare the time. As yet, I have seen so little of the city, and I would appreciate a guided tour."

I glance up at mother to see if I may have misheard and witness an expression on her face I have never seen before. The incredulous joy lighting her eyes is making her appear a woman half her age.

And when my gaze rolls slowly to Lawrie and his own eager expression, I think that this very morning my luck may have turned. For the first time my heart is hammering in my chest for all the right reasons.

For however long it may last, it seems I have bagged myself the most handsome prince in the kingdom.

Chapter 5
1923—Lawrie

Clayton is the perfect village to live the quiet life. I've been seeking an antidote to my busy role at work, and finally we found it.

Built in 1868, the stone cottage topped with a thatched roof sits next to the vicarage and is set back from the roadside. The pathway to the front door is lined with loud pink roses and lavender, with just a smattering of white gypsophila to contrast. I can take no credit for the glorious planting which compliments the house in summertime; Arthur, our gardener comes twice a week to cut the lawn and see to such things.

To think Constance and I have been married three years already, I can hardly believe it. Work is no longer the 'be all and end all' it once was. A sense of home has eluded me my whole life until now and I can't wait to return on an evening.

Constance will be waiting with an icy gin and tonic now summer has arrived, and we will sit and chat about the events of our day before a leisurely evening meal prepared and served by Mrs Osmond. She will then leave us to enjoy our evening alone, the perfect arrangement for us.

Once a welcome distraction or a necessary foothold on the ladder to success, the nights I must attend a work function are now a nuisance. I mostly attend unaccompanied as the social grind is not for

Constance, I knew this before we married, and it's never been a problem for me.

Having thought on occasion that domesticity would be a drudge, I admit now I am a man who is nothing if content. However, I don't take my contentment for granted, nursing a secret fear it may be taken away from me at any moment. Constance thinks losing my parents at a young age may have something to do with it. My mother was never well after having me and she died when I was six, so my memories of her are sparse and hazy. I then lost my father to tuberculosis at seventeen. He was in a sanatorium for almost a year, and I was unable to visit, but this paved the way for my new life as a young orphan, albeit well-provided for. Textiles were our bread and butter for generations, but when I came of age, I sold the mill, only too glad to use the funds to support my choice of career. Textiles in the raw sense were never going to excite me enough to drag me into the office day after day, so I was sensible enough to seek out a buyer. I knew it was the right thing to do and I have not once regretted the decision.

My parent's photograph sits inside my wallet, and I take it out to scrutinise from time to time as though I might spot something different to look at. From the worn image, I can see that my mother was as small-boned and delicate as my father described her, whilst he was tall and strapping. I have my mother's colouring and my father's build, so I comfort myself they are not gone forever. I only wish they could have met Constance; something tells me they would have admired my choice of wife with her sweet and gentle nature.

Perhaps my fear of loss is not unusual, and it may be a good thing to appreciate what we have when it's there under our noses. I've lost my sense of longing for something else, something unknown because now I've found it.

I wondered if Constance might be lonely out here, after the lively community of Hunslet and working at the foundry. I was mistaken, as she too is happy with the solid home life we have built between us. Timothy brings her mother every Thursday evening to join us for our evening meal, and between times she reads or paints, delighted to show me her progress each evening. I am no art expert, but I consider her to be very talented, even without the generous eye of a husband.

I often thank my lucky stars for our interlude that morning in the chemist. We plan, we worry about our fate, but everything happens exactly when it should.

Before Constance there were quite a few women vying for my attention to the point of it making me uncomfortable. I was sketchy about my heritage at university, not wishing to portray myself as the wealthy playboy when I was still recovering from the death of my father. Before and after the war, women seemed to be chasing me wherever I turned and perhaps I began to enjoy the attention for a while at least. The war years were brutal … and lonely.

Then a young woman fainted at my feet.

That Sunday in July when I returned to see Constance after our initial meeting, I knew I had found the missing piece in my life… and where I least expected. She is very beautiful, but it goes far deeper than that. I gave it plenty of thought, realising eventually what I felt was happening between us: She simply completes me. I am a better man because of her.

"Piffle," Kenneth said when I foolishly confessed this to him one night after one too many brandies. "What can someone from such a background offer you? You have been swayed by the thrill of an earthier, more down-to-earth girl, that's all it is. A change is as good as a rest, Lawrie, but it doesn't mean we have to stick with it forever."

I considered my friend as though I was seeing him for the first time. Had he always been such a snob I wondered. What a terrible description of Constance who, like her mother, is nothing if not a lady despite their limited means.

"So, you shall only marry a woman with money, is that what you're saying, Kenneth?"

He ran a hand through his unruly ginger hair, patently irritated by my challenge.

"It's not just about money for pity's sake, it's about breeding, the meeting of minds. What on earth do you two have in common?"

My laugh was hollow, reflecting the remark wasn't even worthy of a response. I doubt I could ever explain it adequately enough for him to understand when I didn't truly understand myself. Some things are beyond comprehension. I drew a long breath.

"It's difficult to put into words how Constance makes me feel, Kenneth, perhaps it's something you need to experience. Suffice to say that we're on the same wavelength, I can reassure you of that at least."

Kenneth and I lost touch after the wedding. It wasn't a deliberate decision, only a mutual understanding we were both happy to abide by.

One of the places Constance showed me on that first Sunday was the *Hope Foundry* where she and her late father worked. I tipped my head back to look at the deserted building, the name etched in stone on the impressive entranceway. I pictured the flurry of activity it would have the day after when the workers returned from their weekend.

"You must miss your father," I said without giving too much thought to the statement. It seemed an appropriate comment to make under the circumstances.

She stood at my side; her head tipped backwards the same as mine.

"He was more than a father," she said quietly.

Something in her tone made me want to turn my head to look at her or link my fingers with hers, but I knew that would have been unacceptable. It was too early in our acquaintance, but I was familiar with such a loss. I could sense her pain.

She remained in the same position for so long, my neck ached, and I had no idea what to do or say for once.

Finally, she dropped her head to glance up at me shyly. She saw something behind my eyes, a mutual understanding I think, and it led to me telling her about my parents as we strolled on through the streets of Hunslet in the sunshine.

That was the day I knew Constance Crawford was mine … and I was utterly hers.

On 25th September, the night of her twenty-second birthday I asked Constance to marry me. I took her to the *City Varieties*, and when I dropped her at the back door of her house as was our usual custom by then, I bent one knee to the cold cobbles and held out a small box. Inside nestled my mother's engagement ring, polished and resized with a little help from her own mother with regard to measurements.

Constance clasped her hand to her mouth and tears sprang in her eyes. It wasn't what I was expecting at all, she looked positively distraught.

"But ... but my hair!" she blurted into the night air.

My eyes went straight to the blonde hairpiece she'd taken to wearing by then.

"What of your hair, Constance? You know how much I love you," I said, "I'm not marrying your hair now, am I? If I was, it would indeed be a very dull marriage."

The waiting tears spilled down her face before she flung her arms around my neck.

"I may be getting a little ahead of myself, but I take it that's a 'yes' then," I said, my hands clutching her waist tightly.

"Yes," she whispered in my ear.

I have never felt a love like it until I slipped my mother's ring on her finger. I shed a tear afterwards myself on my way home for the first time since my father's funeral. I might have proposed at the restaurant in Leeds or in the car, but outside Constance Crawford's back door on 25th September 1919 was precisely the right time and place for such an occasion.

When we married on 5th April the following year, I saw it as the day my life truly began in earnest. Any professional success I'd had before then suddenly paled into insignificance.

It was the night I hoped for us to start as we meant to go on.

I'd given it no end of thought before the big day. How could we begin our married life on a fallacy? She couldn't possibly wear her hairpiece forever, nor should she.

That night Constance was wearing a new silk nightgown, the whiteness of it complementing her fair complexion. I pictured her buying it, her mind full of mixed emotions for the time she would wear it.

She was trembling under the covers on a warm night. Our lips found each other, and I was mindful to be tender knowing it was her first time. I wanted it to be a moment for us to cherish always, feeling quite nervous myself at the weight of expectation.

I peeled back the sheet to lay a hand gently on the lace of her breast. She moaned her pleasure, reaching for my face to pull it down to kiss her again, the frisson in the air mounting so we were both panting between kisses. I put my hand under the silk of her nightdress and trailed my forefinger until it circled the top of her thighs. Her legs opened immediately with a wanting, a wanting for me that made me close my eyes, overcome with passion, longing. It may have been her first time, but I shall never forget how she made me feel. The moment between us built, so she called my name loudly into my neck, our bodies moving in harmony.

"Oh, Constance, my love," I groaned. "This moment is like an awakening!"

It was a surprise, almost a proclamation. I was unable to comprehend how being part of her made me feel: Strong, powerful, her ardent protector.

Afterwards she laid on my chest as I stroked her arm. I was building up to the question because I wanted her to feel free to be who she really was with me.

"You must be yourself with me, darling, I promise there's nothing to fear," I whispered.

I raised my head to look at her, but she only buried her face in me.

"I just don't think I can," she said, the words muffled against my chest.

I turned on my side, so we were facing each other and drew a line down her cheek with my forefinger.

"What will be different tomorrow? Surely, we've just shared the most intimate moment a man and wife can share. I don't want you to be afraid to show me when it's not important to me."

Our eyes melted, filled with unspoken words for a moment, her distress plain to see. Finally, she raised her hand to slide the hairpiece to one side, unable still to remove it completely. Her breathing was heavy when she finally took away the barrier between us.

"How brave you are," I said, wiping her tear with my thumb. "Thank you for trusting me enough."

I leant forward, and she met me halfway to touch our lips together. The moment was as poignant as our first kiss.

"You will always be beautiful to me, Constance, whatever happens. Your looks mean so little with regard to the love I feel for you. Your light shines from within and I only hope after tonight you can believe me."

Her kiss consoled me my words had not fallen on deaf ears.

Neither of us think about it any longer and this is how it should be, and what I hoped for.

I turn to wave farewell to Timothy now as I head up the front path to the cottage. He will be back on Monday morning bright and early to take me to work. Constance and I rarely venture out at weekends, but if we do go into Leeds occasionally for shopping or to a restaurant, we take a taxi. Perhaps we might venture there this weekend as I can't remember the last time we did.

The gala I was due to attend at *John Dysons* was cancelled at the eleventh hour and I struggled to hide my delight when Daphne informed me of it.

Opening the front door quietly I step over the threshold onto the tiles of the long hallway. Mrs Osmond will not be here this evening as Constance tells me she's perfectly capable of making herself a meal when she's dining alone. *A Little Bit of Heaven* is playing on the gramophone, the dulcet tones of Ernest R Ball's piano-playing drifting my way as I open the door to the drawing room. I've learned the piece recently on our piano, though I'm a poor imitation.

Constance is sitting on the chaise by the rear window of the sunroom, her back to me, her head bowed. I think she may be reading, so lost in concentration she's unaware that I've joined her in the room. Perhaps she's unable to hear above the music.

She isn't wearing her hairpiece which is unusual in the daytime, but what is more unusual is the sight of her pulling at the few strands of hair she has left. Her head is lowered towards her lap, and I stop in my tracks with alarm when I notice her rocking gently backwards and forwards, backwards, forwards.

It is a disturbing scene, and a shiver slides down my back as I look on in horror at my wife's anguish.

She seems almost deranged as if acting out a part on stage and I wonder how many times she will have been in such a state before. I come home late at least once a week, possibly twice. I grasp a hand to the back of my neck, no clue what my next move should be.

Perhaps I should leave the room to spare her the added distress and shame of knowing I have witnessed such a private moment. I long to comfort her in some way, touch her shoulder or better yet, pull her into my arms, but I fear making her aware of my presence will make matters worse. I could never have imagined witnessing my wife in such torment only moments ago.

The wonderful piano music we enjoy so much now has the same effect on me as fingernails clawing at a blackboard.

I spend too long deliberating, and in the end the dreadful dilemma of how to tackle the tragedy is taken from my hands.

Chapter 6
1930—Daphne

What a dismal Christmas it was.

In hindsight, disclosing my feelings to Lawrie proved appalling timing, but something overcame me, something so unlike me. All I know is, I just could not live the lie a single second longer.

I torture myself by replaying the conversation in my mind, heat rising from my chest to set my cheeks ablaze each time. Yet still I must relive it like a twisted compulsion.

Evidently, I have misread the signals. Somehow, I convinced myself the cracks were showing over the years since he married Constance. He attends every social function alone and barely makes mention of his wife except in passing. Why would she not accompany him to at least the occasional event? Oh, what I wouldn't give to walk into a room on the arm of that spectacular man.

I left work in a daze on Christmas Eve, taking the tram to Headingley then trudging through the snow to make my way back to the flat I share with mother since our move from Bradford. We've tried our best to make the flat homely, and it's much improved, but it's not a patch on where we used to live. We enjoyed sweeping views of moorland for mile upon mile at the rear of the old Victorian house where we rented top floor rooms. Now our only view is a shabby row of houses that are in dire need of refurbishment.

I feel as though we abandoned a silk purse for a sow's ear ... all in the name of love.

A love that does not even exist, at that.

Laughter and gaiety were wafting from *The Oak* pub as I went past, tempting me to go inside a pub unaccompanied for the first time in my life. Enough people were revelling in Christmas frivolity so I could easily have remained invisible.

Home wasn't calling me; I knew mother and George would be waiting for me to return from work so we could all have tea together and begin our celebrations. I knew the whole process would be repeated the following day, then no doubt again on Boxing Day. The thought of it was stifling.

However, I didn't want mother to worry, and it seems my feet knew this and took me home of their own accord.

"Ah, there you are, Daphne," she said when I arrived. She was wearing her Christmas tree pinafore, her white hair freshly set at the hairdressers to last a whole week until it would need setting again. "I thought Mr Armitage had turned into Scrooge, keeping you at work until this hour on Christmas Eve."

George was standing at her shoulder, his broad grin and ruddy complexion showing me he'd had more than one glass of sherry whilst he was waiting for me. He strode towards me with a bunch of mistletoe in his hand, planting a kiss on my cheek.

"Let the festivities begin, Dappy," he said, as mother laughed and clapped her hands at the jolly gesture.

I was thankful then that my well-rehearsed smile appeared right on cue though tears were sitting at the back of my eyes.

George had made a special effort, creaming his hair from his forehead, his dark green jumper sitting smartly over a starched collar and burgundy tie. He had taken leave from the bank until the New Year and would be calling upon us every day as he only lives two streets away. He had requested a transfer from the *Yorkshire Penny Bank* in Bradford to move to Leeds which was granted without fuss as he's such a highly regarded member of staff. He aspires to be a bank manager and I've no doubt he will be one day.

Despite my feelings for Lawrie, I was relieved when George transferred. Sometimes any boyfriend is preferable to having no boyfriend at all.

That evening may well have been predictable; however, Christmas Day did not turn out as anticipated.

It might have begun much the same as always, except this year I awoke to the memory of the previous day's events. The night before when I got into bed I thrashed for some time, weeping quietly into my pillow. I was relieved not to be at work, whilst at the same time wanting desperately to see Lawrie.

Food was far from my priority. Mother cooked our usual breakfast, the majority of which discreetly found its way to the bin when her back was turned. Thankfully, she was far too preoccupied to notice.

George appeared at half-past twelve on the dot with gifts under his arm which we exchanged for our own. More sherry 'jollied things along' as mother says, or at least it did for her and George.

Christmas dinner was an odd affair. George was as quiet as me though I tried for mother's sake to put a brave face on things. He was twitching in his seat and toying with his food whilst exchanging glances with mother. I was in no mood to question his behaviour, deciding to put my best foot forward and ignore it instead.

After dinner, the washing up done, we sat by the fireside with a cup of tea. The afternoon stretched out before us like a great yawning cavern, and I was about to suggest a walk to the park when George cleared his throat.

"Daphne, there's another little gift I've been saving," he said.

Alarm bells immediately started ringing as my eyes darted his way. He got to his feet, my stomach plummeting when he reached a hand in his pocket.

Oh, dear god, this is really happening, I thought. I knew I'd had a lucky reprieve for many a year, but the timing could not have been worse.

His expression was earnest as he knelt on one knee at my feet, his pinched cheeks a sure sign of his nerves.

"It will be thirteen years next year since we met, Daphne. Such a long time and I was hoping you might finally make an honest man of me."

He chuckled at his own joke, holding a tiny, open box at arm's length. The ring was beautiful, but the sparkle was dimmed by my mood.

Mother gasped and I could sense her eyes upon me, anticipating my answer to his question.

My mind was totally devoid of any emotion, numb, as though I'd taken a sleeping pill and was well on my way to a good night's sleep.

"Of course I'll marry you, George," I said immediately.

It was as if someone had nudged me just before I nodded off and had held up a card for me to read aloud.

His eyes widened, jumping up from his knees to hold me to him until my arms slowly took it in turns to curl around his back.

Then he kissed mother's cheek, as she whispered to him, "Nicely done, George," before placing a hand on his forearm.

"Did you know about this?" I asked her, playing along with the cue card.

A grin spreading across her face mother nodded furiously.

"George asked my permission in the … the absence of your father. He's such a gentleman, but then I don't need to tell you that, Daphne."

Being a gentleman is what I admire most about George.

"I know we've talked about it from time to time in the past," George said, "but I had the impression you weren't quite ready to settle down as you enjoyed your work so much. I've had a few sleepless nights fearing rebuke, Daphne, I can tell you. I can't quite believe it; wait until I tell father."

George's voice floated away. What will Lawrie be doing now, I wondered out of the blue. Would he

54

be playing games with his darling little Dora or banging out festive songs on the piano he insisted on learning to play years ago, his family singing along in accompaniment?

My eyes welled as I stared at the happy expressions of my mother and new fiancé. It wasn't George's fault my heart lay elsewhere.

"When do you think we should have the wedding?" George asked. "June was in my mind; a June bride, isn't that what every girl wants to be?"

I'm not a girl, I thought then, I was well on my way to becoming an old maid. No, a June wedding was not flitting about my mind as it should have been.

I was thinking instead that I must pay a little visit to Lawrie's house now my position had changed. I would have preferred to disappear into the mist, but I owed it to Lawrie to tell him face to face I was to be married and therefore would not be returning to work. George had handed me the perfect excuse and my mood lifted slightly at the realisation.

In that moment it would have been nice to consider which style of wedding dress I would choose, or where to hold the big event. I should have chatted about the colour of the flowers or perhaps the catering, even though the guest list would be minimal to say the least. I happen to know mother has been saving towards my wedding day since I was born.

She and George prattled away with enough excitement for all of us, while I was thinking that a trip to see Lawrie at home would nicely serve the table at both ends for me.

Chapter 7
1923—Constance

The piano music stops, my ears adjusting to the silence.

I swing around in my seat when I suddenly hear heavy breathing behind me. Lawrie is just … standing there, his hand swinging helplessly by his side, his other hand on the back of his neck.

His face is the colour of the net curtains Mrs Osmond bleached on the line in the sunshine earlier. His brown eyes are misted as he tries and fails to hold my gaze which is winging around the room like a demented fly. I jump up from the chaise, caught now by my husband in what I imagine must appear a disturbing act. I wasn't expecting him to be home for hours.

Once I would never have imagined letting Lawrie see me without my hairpiece. Once I would never have believed I would allow my handsome husband to look upon my thinning hair, the thought bringing me to tears. But he convinced me that it didn't matter to him, not in the slightest. After our wedding night, I wavered from my belief a little, but in time I settled; one cannot fake these things. Lawrie has convinced me it really doesn't affect how he loves me, desires me even.

However, I'm not a fool. I'm aware this could change, that what I consider my house of cards could be blown down by a breath of wind, especially as children are still not part of our lives. We've waited three long years and oh, how we long for them.

Many women would love to whisk Lawrie away given even a whiff of opportunity, Daphne Farrington being top of the list. I dare not mention it in case I sow a seed on this barren ground. Barren for now at least.

So, my deepest, darkest fears have been put on display, lined up for him to see in all their cruel glory.

"You're home early, Lawrie," I say, stating the obvious, trying to overlook the distress tumbling from his eyes. He ignores the statement.

"Constance, why didn't you tell me?" he asks. "Your pain is raw; I see it so clearly."

His arms reach towards me, but I shy away, desperately seeking to avoid the conversation. I must find my hairpiece. He follows me, so I pick up speed, dashing from the sitting room and down the hallway. I wipe a tear from my cheek, my pace quickening to almost a run, the clickety-clack of his footsteps on the tiles trying to keep up, giving me the horrid sensation of being chased.

He catches me, tugging my elbow to turn me around to face him as I'm trying to wriggle frantically from the hook.

"Darling, you're… you're not well," he stumbles over his choice of words. "I suspected you had a nervous condition, but I see now it goes far beyond that. Please, I want to help you; you must let me help you."

A sob echoes around us and I realise it has escaped from me. I free my arm to slump like a rag doll onto the tiles, my back to the wall. I have no energy to engage in this discussion, one which I was not expecting. I'm not strong enough.

His feet, still in his shiny work shoes, step towards me like the day in mother's parlour when we met. Wrapping my skirt around my legs I drop my head to my knees. I cannot look up or his wounded puppy dog eyes will be my complete undoing.

"How can you love me as you do, Lawrence?" I ask, my voice almost a wail, smothered in my skirts.

I'm startled as two hands grip my upper arms gently but firmly and hoist me to my feet. Still my chin sits near my chest.

"Constance, please, look at me," he says quietly, a note of desperation hidden in his request.

The hallway is silent, but for the magnified sound of our heaving breaths. I'm still unable to bring myself to look at my husband.

"Please, darling, look at me!"

His tone forces me to glance up but only briefly. His glistening eyes are too much to bear, so I set my eyes on his tie instead, the one I bought him two birthdays ago. I always buy him a tie and he always buys me something luxurious and wonderful; it's become our little joke.

"Do you think our love is so brittle I would think differently of you because you're unwell? I told you before we married and since, there is no-one; *no-one* who has come close to making me feel the way I do about you. I thought I'd convinced you of the sincerity of my love, but it seems that I've failed."

His voice breaks and I gasp, his words stinging as if he's struck me. I've been selfish, thinking only of my own regrets and insecurities and not how hard he's tried to shower his devotion on me.

I slide my arms around his neck, my eyes searching his face. He's still even now trying to hide his pain from me.

"You mustn't think you've let me down, Lawrie," I whisper. "How could you have known what I was going through when I've convinced everyone, my own mother even, that I've come to terms with my affliction?"

His eyes finally meet mine head on.

"I should be the one you turn to; I wanted you to feel safe enough in our marriage to unmask your demons. We all have them, every one of us."

I wonder what demons he might be hiding in that tidy mind of his. Do they lurk still, or are they gone?

He strokes my wet cheek with his thumb, a question sitting in his eyes, so I brace myself.

"Is there anything else you need to tell me?"

My breath catches and holds fast. I'm not ready. Some words have never passed my lips before and they can't be prized or even coaxed out, not today.

"I'd like to sit down," I say. "Perhaps you might fix us a drink. I just need to powder my nose and then I'll join you in the back garden so we can enjoy the last of today's sunshine."

His arms drop to his sides, staring at me too long. I wonder if he thinks I might bolt out of the back door and run away.

"I shan't be a minute," I say, attempting a smile to placate him.

His eyes follow me with each step as I make my way upstairs.

I sit at my dressing table, forcing myself to look at my reflection. Usually, I make sure my hairpiece is in place before I set my makeup, but today I must look at myself for the first time in years. I must see what my husband sees each morning.

I may have disguised it well in public, but privately I've been floundering, ever since what happened to father. The doctor saw it all those years ago and if nothing else the events of this evening have shown me the problem has become worse.

"What am I doing?" I murmur in the quiet of our bedroom, dropping my head on my forearm to sob tears I have been holding onto for too long. They have been scorching my insides, much like the unspoken words about things I simply could not speak of tonight.

I squirrel the box of monogrammed cufflinks back into the rear of Lawrence's draw, the one with the tiny label on the back bearing the name *John Dyson Fine Jewellers*, the same jewellers Lawrence and Daphne have longstanding connections with. They are new and I know that Gregory wouldn't have bought them for him, nor would Lawrence ever buy himself such a gift. Even if he had, he would have showed them to me, or more importantly, worn them.

My worst fears are coming true. So now the haunting question is, will I ever be able to stop the ride so I can get off by myself … or will Daphne Farrington be the one to come up behind me and push me off?

Chapter 8
1930—Daphne

The guard opens the door and I step from the train, my breath curling into the cold air. The relief of finally being free of the city and the oppressive atmosphere of home is tangible.

I telephoned work this morning from the telephone box on the corner of Brook Street to make my excuses. Beryl answered the telephone having drawn the short straw with the Christmas rota this year. I informed her I had a head cold, so I would be off work for a few days. This is highly irregular as I have never taken time off for any reason.

"Oh, Ms Farrington, you shouldn't have come out in this weather, you should have asked your mother to call," Beryl said, tugging the thread of my conscience. "You sound dreadful; go home and tuck yourself up in bed with a cup of extra-sweet tea and a hot stone."

I thanked Beryl for her concern and sloped off to have three cups of tea in three different cafés as I waited for the quarter past two train. I had no intention of going home to sit with mother and George for yet another never ending day of deceit.

Mother had been eager to make a start on wedding plans. I wasn't as surprised as she might have imagined as I'd seen a receipt from *Frobisher's,* by far the finest jewellers in Leeds, peeping out from

George's wallet. I only caught a glimpse of the distinctive insignia but it's the place where a man would buy the best engagement ring should he want to impress his ladylove. Was this why I responded to his proposal almost without thinking? No doubt George saw this as a sign of my eagerness when in reality it was an act of cold, hard survival following Lawrie's rejection.

Unwittingly, he had picked the perfect moment to propose.

How lucky Lawrie is to live in this beautiful countryside, I think now. He was delighted to find the "perfect" home to start their married life after months of searching. I've never set eyes on the house, though I've pictured it in my mind's eye many times over the years. I even imagined myself baking in the kitchen or sitting with him by the fireside on occasion; all whimsical pipedreams it turns out now.

I have only myself to blame. There was ample opportunity to confess my feelings to Lawrie when we were working late into the evening or even when sharing a ride home slightly tipsy in his car after a work function. Sometimes Timothy would catch my eye through the rear-view mirror, and I sensed he thought our connection odd.

Many opportunities sailed by. I blame mother for instilling in me that a lady should never make the first move with a man under any circumstances.

"Remember, a lady must bide her time to catch her man's eye, Daphne. There are certain wiles we can use to prompt this, of course, but we must always be subtle about it."

That plan did not work with Lawrie. He never noticed the efforts I made with my appearance, the perfume I wore, the way I lingered after placing his teacup on his desk. It was all lost on him as though he didn't even see me as a woman, and an attractive woman at that. I've been called attractive enough times, though I say so myself; George even referred to me as beautiful once.

Twilight has descended as I step onto the empty platform, thankful the snow has been cleared so the conditions underfoot are not so perilous by the train tracks. Nobody else gets off at Clayton, so I'm left alone as the train pulls away into the gloom, wondering if being here proves I've lost my mind. I am losing my nerve, but the next and last return train is in two hours so I will have a long time to sit and reflect in the waiting room. I peer through the window and see a fire still blazing in the hearth but still this is not enough to draw me inside and waylay me from my mission.

My shoulders rise and fall, and I take the first step of my onward journey with a sigh of resolution. There will never be another opportunity to visit the house I've longed to see.

There was no need to write down the address as I know it by heart: *Hawthorne Cottage, No. 17 Wood Lane, Clayton, West Yorkshire.*

I laid in bed last night formulating my plan. I don't imagine him living in a small house, so I assume it will be on the main road through the village.

The chill wind makes me push my fur collar further towards my chin. I decided that my best outdoor ensemble of a bottle-green coat with a brown collar and matching fur hat would be a suitable look for today. My new crocodile skin bag was a Christmas gift from mother and my brown fur-topped snow boots complete my smart attire. I donned the pieces one by one almost ceremoniously this morning, hoping they might instil me with confidence. Mother enquired why I was so dressed up and I'd already thought of the excuse. There is to be an after-work fuddle for the staff I told her, and she told me to have a nice time and she would forgo preparing any supper for me.

That was my first little white lie of the day.

The store was closing earlier today, so Lawrie will have been home an hour or so by now. Wood Lane is the third street sign I spot, and I give myself a pat on the back for my excellent detective skills.

I walk some four hundred yards or so before I spot No.15, the house next door to Lawrie. The houses have high walls and are set back from the road, with most curtains still to be drawn. The glowing Christmas tree lights from the windows is a pretty sight in the fading light.

The sign for *Hawthorne Cottage* is engraved in brass, freshly polished and shining against the stone of the wall. The word 'cottage' is misleading as it looks to be a far grander residence, perfect in size, not too large nor too small. There's a burning lantern hanging above the door and mullion glass in the windowpanes. Smoke from the chimney wisping into the semi-gloom completes the picturesque scene. I can certainly see why Lawrie chose this house, why the journey into the city and back each weekday is worth it.

Should I go any further, I wonder as I peer through the gaps in the high wrought-iron gate. I have not been invited to enter the kingdom that lies beyond these gates and an uninvited guest is always a nuisance, though people are keen to pretend otherwise.

The thickening air burns my chest as my breathing becomes more laboured. I must remember that a telephone call will not suffice after all the years we have worked side by side.

Lifting the latch, the gate moans as I open it and I wait a moment to see if anyone appears. When stillness remains, I step onto the pathway through a wintry garden. Twenty-eight steps lead me to a large and imposing front door. I pause briefly and then ring the bell before stepping back onto the gravel as I wait.

At the very moment I glance upwards, a face like a startled rabbit appears briefly in the bottom corner of the bedroom window. I wouldn't have noticed had I not been looking; intruding now feels a better description. I return my eyes swiftly to the front door, unsettled by Constance's expression. This does not bode well for the conversation which lies ahead.

The housekeeper opens the door, her black dress a contrast to her pristine white apron and cap. Her shoes are flat and sensible almost like a man's shoe.

"May I help you, madam," she enquires now, her eyes fixed firmly on mine. Her tone is neither unpleasant nor cordial, only professionally warm. I perfected the tone well myself.

"You must be Mrs Osmond," I say. "My name is Farrington, Ms Daphne Farrington; I am Mr Armitage's assistant. I'm sorry to impose, but I was hoping I might be able to have a brief word with him on an urgent matter?"

She inclines her head slightly opening the door wider. The first hurdle over with, I'm now pleased to discover Mrs Osmond is too polite to enquire as to the nature of my visit, only inviting me to step inside.

"If you will wait here a moment, I shall be right back, Miss … Ms Farrington," she says as I enter the hallway.

The warmth of the house seeps through my coat as I wait, wondering if Constance will appear at the top of the staircase. Lawrie will no doubt be bewildered as to why I'm here, especially as I'm supposed to be unwell. Perhaps he realises it was a ruse and I'm taking extra time to recover after my declaration of love. I'm certain he will see me as he would not wish to raise alarm bells with his wife or his housekeeper.

A childish voice drifts from the sitting room as the door opens then closes. I imagine Mrs Osmond quietly telling Lawrie of his visitor, then the drop of his face as he digests the name.

He appears now to the rear of Mrs Osmond, his face split by a broad smile, one which appears to be genuine. Mrs Osmond takes my coat and hat before heading to the kitchen and closing the door quietly behind her without a backward glance. All is calm, all is bright, suddenly springs to mind.

Lawrie and I now find ourselves alone. I search for my well-rehearsed words but they elude me.

"Ms Farrington, what a surprise, Beryl informed me you had a head cold this morning," he says, a quizzical note in his voice. "You must be frozen in this weather. Please, come through to the sitting room and warm yourself by the fire."

He steps to one side, extending his hand by way of invitation. I almost scoot past him, glancing up at the staircase as I go.

Dora interrupts her playing on the hearth rug with what looks to be a brand, spanking new teddy bear with a tartan bow and a child's tea set. I return her bright smile with stretched lips; I was expecting to speak to her father alone.

"Dora, this is Ms Farrington a lady I work with. Please will you go upstairs and tell mummy we have a visitor? Perhaps she's refreshed enough from her nap to join us."

She tucks teddy bear under her arm as she joins me.

"How do you do?" she asks politely, with a small curtsey. She turns to her father before I can answer. "Daddy, does this mean we'll be having tea early now?"

Lawrie smiles fondly at his daughter, her dark curls in a ponytail reaching the bow sitting on her waist at the rear of her dress. Her eyes are wide with anticipation.

"We shall be having refreshments with our guest, yes, but surely you're not hungry already after the huge luncheon Nanny O made us."

Dora gives him a charming little grin, before heading out of the room on her errand.

She has her father's colouring and her mother's delicate build. It's hardly any wonder Lawrie's expression is positively glowing with pride when she's such a dear little thing.

He turns his attention to me.

"Please, do sit down, Ms Farrington," he says, his smile lingering but I somehow don't feel the warmth is directed at me. "I apologise, my daughter can be quite a distraction at times."

He doesn't seem flustered nor even a little irritated by my sudden appearance on his doorstep. There's no indication of coyness or being wrong-footed in any way. In fact, if it wasn't for his more casual attire, he seems to be the same sanguine Lawrence of old. Perhaps his ploy is to pretend our conversation never took place.

I perch on the far end of the brocade sofa. The room has an air of opulence, but then he isn't short of a bob or two as George likes to remind me.

He offers me a cigarette from a silver box, but I decline, not being much of smoker unless I feel it's necessary to fit in at a social event. He returns the holder to the side table without lighting a cigarette himself, then sits in the larger of the two chairs by the fireside. I tear my gaze away from the smaller chair; it seems almost symbolic of Constance's imminent arrival.

"So, to what do I owe the pleasure?" he asks as though I regularly pop in for a cup of tea and fireside chat.

Apparently, tonight's theme will be business as usual and sweeping everything under the carpet. As the silence swaddles me, I realise I've been studying him too long. I clear my throat, sitting up straight on full alert, and wishing now I had accepted the offer of the cigarette, if only for something to do with my hands.

"Well, firstly, I must apologise for intruding on your home, especially at such a late hour and unannounced, Mr Armitage," I say. "However, I'm afraid I had no alternative as I thought it only polite to inform you in person of an unexpected turn of events." I pause for dramatic effect. "With regret, I must terminate my employment with *Lewis's* … with immediate effect."

His eyes widen slightly, and I can't help a touch of satisfaction at finally drawing a reaction.

"Might I ask why? It just seems rather sudden. I hope …"

I race to cut him off.

"Yesterday I received an offer of marriage and … and I was only too pleased to accept."

His brow furls then his dear eyes widen before he jumps from his seat to shake my hand. He places his second hand on top of mine, and I lean into the comfort of his cordial embrace briefly.

"Well, well, this is good news. May I be one of the first to congratulate you on your forthcoming marriage to Mr Jackson. I'm delighted for you both."

His reaction makes my heart plummet like a pebble in a stream, made worse by him knowing who holds my true affection.

The door opens and I expect to see Constance with perhaps Dora, but instead Mrs Osmond arrives with the tea tray. She sets it down on the low table, pouring two cups before turning to Lawrie. I spot a third cup and saucer.

"Mrs Armitage said to tell you she will be down in a moment to join you, sir," she says.

He thanks her with far more warmth than one might usually extend to a servant. She dips her knee and leaves us alone once more.

"Shamefully, after all the tea you have made me, I'm afraid I have no idea how you take your own tea," he says.

He hands me a cup, and I add some milk and one sugar. I have no thirst for it, only a desire to leave and seek refuge in the station waiting room. I've done what I came to do; seen what I came to see.

"I confess, Ms Farrington, I'm disappointed you feel you must leave your post immediately," he says, his eye on his teacup. "I was hoping you might stay on at least until the wedding."

He's disappointed; disappointed he says, yet what alternative do I have? I only want to extricate myself from this agonising conversation. I was foolish to let curiosity get the better of me.

"There will be so much to do for the wedding. I … I think I will be too busy to give my job the attention it needs and deserves," I say, stirring my tea.

He runs a hand through his hair, the waves bouncing back into place like the intrusion never happened.

"You see, I rather think you might be leaving too hastily and for the wrong reasons. I'd hate to think I was the one who drove you from you job early when I know how much it means to you."

His eyes meet mine briefly before I turn away from the softness of them. It was his eyes that first made me fall in love with him; so deep and expressive to magnify his thoughts.

"Won't you reconsider?" he asks quietly. "I know you will be leaving, but there's no need to run away. I think we are both professional enough to maintain an appropriate working relationship. Don't you agree?"

I realise now what a mistake this visit was and how deluded my expectations have become. I had been living in cloud cuckoo land thinking he might ask me to reconsider my marriage proposal, if only because he knew I could not possibly be in love with George. But to Lawrence I now know for certain, I am merely a loyal hardworking colleague; matters of my heart would be of no concern to him.

However, he may be right about one thing: Perhaps leaving my post immediately is not the answer, perhaps it is a ludicrous overreaction. I would indeed be running away like a child.

Perhaps, above all else I'm unable to leave him behind just yet.

I made my excuses and left Lawrie's beautiful home before my tea was cold and finished. I'm sure he will have been relieved to see me go, and I was left in no doubt about exactly where I stood in his life.

There was nothing more to be said or discussed. We agreed that I would be leaving my job when I was ready but not before. Lawrence is nothing if not benevolent and fair-minded.

My tears had to wait a long time. They remained elusive throughout the walk back to the train station, in the waiting room, on the train home, while I was sitting with mother telling lies about my day, until I was finally in the seclusion of my bedroom. Then thoughts of Lawrie telling his wife my 'good news' before continuing their cosy evening broke my heart, so I thought it might never be mended. Any hope I had carried around with me had fallen from my grasp and shattered.

And all the while I was at *Hawthorne Cottage*, Constance Armitage never made an appearance … and it didn't surprise me, not in the slightest.

Chapter 9
1923—Constance

I'm lifted clean off my feet and swung around in the arms of my husband, unable to help myself from laughing with joy and careless abandon.

"At last, it's finally happened for us. I told you we only had to be patient for the little cherry on our cake. And here's me, thinking I was getting a tie."

My feet touch the ground, but Lawrie leaves his arms around my waist, staring into the deepest part of me as is his want. I appreciate the sensation sometimes more than others; today I am melted to the core by it.

"I'm so happy, Constance," he murmurs almost to himself. "I thought I might be asking too much when I have so much already."

If only he knew I'd been plagued by the same shameful thoughts of feeling greedy for wanting more. I discard the memory, determined not to spoil this special moment.

Four years we have been waiting for this celebration. I decided to wait a little longer until Lawrie's birthday to tell him he is to become a father. I could not imagine a better gift.

"When?" he asks, pulling me by the hand to sit beside him on the settee.

"May; early summer, surely the perfect time to have a baby. Next year will be wonderful for us, Lawrie, I sense it."

Shaking his head, a thoughtful smile appears as he strokes the back of my hand with his thumb. Soon the questions he is waiting to ask will be unleashed. Already I know there will be some I would prefer not to answer.

"Has Dr Fitzpatrick assured you all is well so far?" he asks.

Too soon the doctor has been mentioned. I was hoping for a brief reprieve at least.

"Yes, all is as it should be, Lawrie, don't fret. You can allow yourself the opportunity to bask in this long-awaited moment."

He tilts his face to look at me, but I turn to stare at the fire roaring up the back of the grate. He will know the remark was meant to prevent him from probing any further.

"Timothy will be dropping mother shortly. I think I shall just check on supper," I say. "Mrs O has made you a birthday cake. It's a beauty, she really went to town with the decoration."

I make a move to get up from my seat, but my hand is not released from his grip. He has been patient long enough. I close my eyes knowing I'm to face an inquisition whether I would like to or not.

"Constance, this is difficult for me to say but I must; it must be now, or I will lose my nerve. I haven't pushed you on this matter for over a year, not since I discovered the extent of your… your distress. I know we have spoken of it on occasion, and you assure me all is well." His hand tightens. "I'm afraid though I remain unconvinced. I wonder now if under the circumstances we should look at a satisfactory way forward for us."

I pull my hand sharply and scrabble to my feet. Oh, how I have tried to put the past behind me, to hide the extent of my pain, but I knew this day would come and I've dreaded it. I put a hand to my forehead realising that leaving the room will be useless as he will only follow me.

"Please, Constance, we must also think now of the baby. You need to be strong to cope with the demands of pregnancy and motherhood."

A prickling sensation appears on the nape of my neck. Whether the sensation is from fear or irritability is immaterial; he is still sullying the wonderful moment I've taken great pains to create for us.

"Lawrie, I don't wish to be unkind but what would you know about the demands of pregnancy and motherhood?"

I turn away from his wounded expression. Instead, I study the oil painting by the window. What was a mere hobby for me has found several admirers in the local art world since Gregory took an interest in a watercolour Lawrie displays in his office. Right at this moment, I should like to step onto the moorland, to lay back and hide amongst the sweeping mounds of heather.

I know he always has my best interests at heart, and I love him dearly for it. But surely, tonight is not the night to discuss a way forward, whatever that means and entails.

He appears in front of me and tries to take my hands. The last thing I want is to hold his hands as then I will be ensnared. I turn swiftly and head to the kitchen.

Mrs Osmond is startled by my sudden entrance into her domain. I rarely interfere with her work, and she puts the pan hastily down on the range to almost stand to attention. I'm now as trapped here as I was in the sitting room.

"It's not quite ready, madam. I'm sorry I didn't hear the bell," she says.

We have a more than cordial but less than friendly relationship. I'm fond of our housekeeper, but also glad she doesn't live-in. Lawrie is used to staff whereas I still feel a little unsure how to act in her presence.

"Please don't worry, I only came to check we have everything in hand as mother is due shortly."

The sound of the car door shutting is right on cue, though she's early. Thank heavens, I think as I rush to the front door to greet my mother. She will serve me nicely as protection from further interrogation this evening.

Mother appears wearing a new fox fur stole, her hair set by the hairdresser. Lawrie will be touched she's made an extra-special effort for him.

"Good evening, mother. I'm so happy you could join us to celebrate," I say.

Her brows knits at my formal greeting, pulling her head back slightly before closing the door behind her.

"Constance, are you quite alright, you look rather flushed? Don't tell me you're coming down with a chill." She doesn't wait for a response. "Have you told Lawrie the wonderful news?"

"Yes, and he's over the moon as one might expect," I say, taking her stole.

Mrs Osmond appears her face aglow from the heat of the kitchen.

"Ah, hello there, Gladys," mother says, handing me her jacket and straightening the collar of her silk blouse, "I see my daughter is snatching your job from under your nose this evening."

They share a chuckle as they often do. They're both similar in age and backgrounds so have much in common.

"Is that my favourite mother-in-law I hear?" Lawrie calls.

She beams before rushing into the living room.

"You little charmer, Lawrence. Happy birthday to my favourite son-in-law. I hope you have a sherry waiting for me."

He bends for her to plant a kiss on both his cheeks, and they smile fondly at each another. Lawrie has missed a mother in his life, and he has embraced his relationship with mine. I know he visits her alone from time to time, which I imagine is a little unusual in most families.

"I can go one better tonight, mother," I say. "I have some champagne which Mrs Osmond has kindly put on ice for the double celebration."

"A double celebration indeed, Lawrie, warm congratulations on impending fatherhood. My daughter and grandchild could not be in better hands."

Lawrie draws her to his side and kisses the top of her forehead. The most important people in my life are overcome with happiness, whilst I feel as though an elephant has me pinned to the ground with one foot on my chest.

I pull the cord and Mrs Osmond appears with the champagne bucket. I intend to tell her my news tomorrow; this evening is just for the family.

Over dinner, I pepper mother with banal questions, hoping to keep the atmosphere light.

"Constance, I ask you again, are you quite alright? You don't seem yourself at all," she asks finally.

I steal a glance at Lawrie. His face is set but his expression soft making my eyes flee and I take a long drink of water.

"Constance is a little upset with me, mother," Lawrie says quietly.

She glances at us in turn and puts down her dessert fork.

"I see. Can your disagreement not wait until tomorrow?" she asks me.

"I'm sorry, it's me who's putting a dampener on our celebrations but unfortunately, we now have a deadline," he says. "I would like Constance to seek help for her condition. You must understand, it doesn't trouble me, but I know how distressed it makes Constance. Now we have our child to think of and I'd like her to be well before the baby arrives."

I'm horrified that he should be so carelessly candid. I throw my napkin on the table and scrape my chair back to flee the dining room, but as I do mother touches my arm. It's by no means an affectionate touch, I'm sure she only wishes to detain me.

But now there are tears in her eyes, and I see something behind them she has never shown me before. It is telling me a story.

"You know, don't you, you know about Lawrie finding me in a state that night?" I ask, my throat narrowing to try to strangle the words before they are out. My face turns towards my husband who is staring at his half-eaten cake.

"Lawrence, how could you?" I whisper. "That was a private moment, just between the two of us."

He can't look at me but even as I know the evening is ruined, I'm also aware he has been battling his own anxiety for too long.

I pull away from mother so fiercely her ring grazes my forearm making me take a sharp intake of breath, but she's too preoccupied to notice.

"Constance, a husband has every right to be concerned about his wife's welfare especially when a situation has showed no sign of improvement for many a year."

I look between the two of them, Lawrie's pallor as pale as my mother's is flushed. I can't sit here any longer. As I dash from the room and towards the stairs, I catch Mrs Osmond's look of alarm as she's stands at the kitchen doorway drying her hands. This night has turned from what should have been one of the best to one of the worst of my life.

I take the stairs too rashly until I remember my condition.

Now, with each step I take away from the persecution I've faced in my own front room, I'm thinking that it will be a cold day in hell before I deign to take marital advice from my mother.

Chapter 10
1930—Lawrie

"Can I have a moment of your time, Mr Armitage?" Daphne asks as I hang up my hat and jacket on the stand.

I'm only too pleased to be facing away as my eyes close of their own accord. Business has been the only item on the agenda between us these last four months since she came to my home. This simple request now has a ring of the personal about it, so I feel I must brace myself.

I was in such a light mood on the drive into work, basking in the memory of early morning. It's been a while since Constance and I woke to find each other in the same frame of mind and I admit it was a pleasant surprise. Her hand reached behind her back to grasp what she was craving, whispering she'd had a dream about the two of us making love. I pushed myself against her so she could be in no doubt about the power she has over me, then lifted her nightgown to slide inside her. She gasped before groaning into the folds of her pillow, mindful not to wake Dora. The pleasure was a welcome start to the day.

I know she doubts it still, but Constance has something nobody else has. It might be just as difficult to define, I only know I cherish it more as the years pass. I'd left the house with a warm glow, as she waved me off to work. I hoped to carry the memory around with me all day as our shared little secret. Now though I suspect the memory is to be shooed away in the next few moments.

"Of course, please step into my office, Ms Farrington," I say.

As I sit down with the barrier of my desk now firmly reinstalled between us, the absence of her notepad means my suspicions are correct and this is to be a tricky conversation. Her usually busy hands sit firmly clasped on her lap instead.

"So, what is it you wish to discuss?" I ask, reaching for an amiable tone.

Her head lowers, her chest rising as she takes a breath. Is she about to tender her notice early I wonder? I presumed she would be working for at least another two months until just before the date of the wedding.

"This is rather difficult for me," she says. The muscles of my stomach clench. "I'm … I'm afraid I find myself in a predicament." She pauses to swallow and compose herself. "One not of my own choosing."

Of the many scenarios playing in my mind, the obvious conclusion is that she's to have a baby a little earlier than planned. I like to think I'm a man of the world and suspect this isn't unusual. In any case the wedding is in less than two months, a little white lie surely wouldn't be out of the question.

"I see," I say levelly.

"I'm going to have a baby," she almost splutters, her eyes still fixed to the carpet.

I wonder why she feels the need to confess her situation to me of all people when the timing of a baby's arrival can be brushed over or explained away.

I stare at her crestfallen face, her burning cheeks, and try to find a suitable response.

"I'm aware the timing is a little off kilter however I'm delighted for you and Mr Jackson."

I thought we'd made an unspoken pact to stick to business matters, hoping I'd made my position clear. We almost seemed to have regained the status quo, and I sensed we were starting to relax a little into the steady, comfortable professional rhythm we had before. Perhaps it was only my perception.

Her eyes meet mine finally and I can clearly see there's far more to this revelation than I anticipated.

"George, Mr Jackson, has called off the wedding," she says. "I regret to have to inform you that he no longer wishes to marry me."

She pulls a crumpled handkerchief from her sleeve, one which shows evidence of being previously used, pressing it to her mouth.

The implication of her words puts an entirely different complexion on matters. A glut of pity settles in the pit of my stomach. A baby appearing less than nine months after the wedding is one thing, a pregnancy outside of marriage entirely another. I feel sorry for her as indeed I would anyone in her situation.

I wonder now why George Jackson would call off the wedding. I only hope he hasn't discovered her true feelings for me at the eleventh hour or I would feel unduly responsible.

"I'm sorry to see you in such a troubling situation, Ms Farrington, sincerely I am."

She smiles weakly, shaking her head.

"Please ... don't be kind, I shan't be able to bear it."

I know how kind words can be one's undoing. It happened to me after my father died when a friend from his army days touched my arm and said what a good man he was and how proud he was of me. A funeral wake with almost a hundred mourners was the most inopportune moment to fall to pieces. It took me almost twenty minutes to re-emerge from the men's room.

"Have you considered he might perhaps change his mind?" I ask now. "Pre-wedding jitters are commonplace, so I hear."

Her lip quivers, giving away her answer.

"No, I'm afraid his mind is set. He has decided to cast me adrift, and after trying on numerous occasions to change his mind, I know I must now accept it. If I thought there was any chance of a reconciliation, I would never have told you."

I've never met her fiancé, but I assumed she would only take up with a gentleman. This is not the behaviour I would expect from a man of honour.

"If you don't mind, Mr Armitage, I would like to work until such a time that the pregnancy can no longer be hidden. I would not wish to sully your reputation or that of *Lewis's* with my predicament."

Heat rising up my neck now, it's as though I'm in front of a roaring fire when the spring weather means no fire is necessary.

"That is not my concern I can assure you. I only wonder what might happen afterwards. How will you survive without money, I understand your mother is quite elderly after all?"

She twists her handkerchief between her fingers without answering the question, perhaps still searching for a solution.

"I have some savings and my mother has a small pension from my late father. I'm afraid one step at a time is all I can manage to think about at present. Informing you of the situation was today's step."

I can't help but feel deep sadness for Daphne Farrington. She absolutely loves her job, and I was surprised she was prepared to sacrifice her career for marriage.

"I wouldn't want to give you the wrong impression," I say after a moment, "but if I can help you at all, I shall."

I surprise myself with the sincerity of my words. Her feelings may be misplaced, but how can we choose who we care for?

As she stands to leave, my eyes stray to her stomach. She places a hand over as though protecting the child within. She clearly has the instincts of a good mother already.

Her secret will cause a scandal of some magnitude should it be found out, yet she will be far from the first or the last for that matter to find herself in this quandary. I shall endeavour to keep her secret as she will need all the money she can get, but eventually this will be impossible unless she's prepared to move away.

But I think perhaps after all these years I owe her my support, for a while at least, as one colleague to another if nothing else.

After Daphne leaves the room, I find myself sitting for some time with my thoughts, mulling over the years we have worked together. Her situation is of her own making, I think and of perhaps devoting herself to her career for too long.

But as I now know, it was not her career she was so devoted to, and I too am responsible for preventing her from having a well-rounded life and a solid relationship.

I pick up my pen to start my day, then place it down again when my heart begins to race at the realisation.

A little peck of guilt has suddenly settled itself in my mind and I admit to finding it decidedly uncomfortable.

Chapter 11
1930—Daphne

I glance up from my magazine to see Josephine Briggs hovering, lunch tray in hand. I'm intrigued why she's keen to sit with me for lunch today but extend a hand of invitation. She promptly joins me at the table, rattling the crockery on the tray in her hurry to sit down.

"Hello, Daphne," she says, settling herself opposite. "It's not long to the wedding now, I should imagine it's all you can think about."

The grin under her freckly nose makes her appear childlike and endearing, almost like a sweet, little cartoon character. She broke quite a few hearts by all accounts when she married last year. I should imagine anytime now she will be announcing she's to have a baby. I can't help feeling a touch of envy that Josephine is sticking to the tried and tested sequence of life events; there will be no rending of garments and gnashing of teeth for her, only a simple, straightforward domestic arrangement.

It's not often I come to the staff canteen, preferring to eat a sandwich at my desk in between tasks. Only this week however I've been feeling the fatigue more, so a break is necessary to get through the working day. I was careful to time my lunch break for when the canteen would be quieter.

I slide the latest edition of *Brides* magazine to one side. The pretence is a pain and an expense I could do without, but appearances must be maintained.

"Yes, I am rather looking forward to the big day," I say. "Even if my to-do list keeps getting longer by the minute."

She leans forward across the table as though she's about to share a confidence. I instinctively pull my head away at the intrusion, but she doesn't notice.

"If there's anything I can do to help, you only need to ask." She pauses then looks down at her plate as she adds lashings of salt to her meal. "Is anybody from here going to the wedding?"

Josephine my dear, you are about as subtle as a sledgehammer, I think. So, that was why she asked to join me for lunch, she's angling for an invitation. An invitation to a fictitious wedding, little does she know.

"No, we've decided it's just going to be a tiny gathering, you know, quite intimate. I prefer those types of weddings as does George."

She sniffs picking up her knife and fork to eat the meat and potato pie on offer today. I couldn't resist the little dig as there's nothing worse than a showy bride, which she undoubtably was. Elegant and understated is more my style … or it would be, given the opportunity.

"How's life treating you on the top floor; any gossip?" she asks before cutting heartily into her pie, her engagement ring twinkling in the light from the canteen window.

Anyone looking on might think we're the best of friends when I've only eaten my lunch with her on two previous occasions. The rest of the time we exchange nothing more than pleasantries when I head down to haberdashery with the pay packets on Friday afternoons.

"You know, you're the envy of the place here, Daphne. We'd all sell our souls to the devil to work for dishy Lawrence Armitage, he's so dreamy. We positively swoon when he walks past the haberdashery counter. He's like one of the leading men we watch on the big screen at *The Regal*."

Her giggle leads to a snort, and I can't help but smile. Lawrie does have an air of the leading man about him, though he has no interest in such things. I know it would come as a surprise to him to hear Josephine's glowing description.

"Don't you think it's funny how we never hear much about his wife?" she asks me now. "She doesn't go anywhere with him from what I gather yet I wouldn't want to let him out of my sight if he was my husband. One of the reasons I picked my Derek was that I didn't need to spend my life looking over my shoulder to check if anyone else was batting their eyelashes at him."

I'm not sure I agree with her strange criteria for a husband. Surely a wife should admire her husband and above all trust him. Derek is quite a few years older than Josephine and he appeared smitten, never leaving her side at the staff Christmas fuddle. On the other hand, she seemed quite indifferent towards him if I recall. Perhaps she's one of *those* women who seek nothing more than babies and security from a marriage.

Baby or no baby I made my decision, I would rather be left on the shelf than marry a man whom I'm unable to respect and admire. Most women, including my mother, would think me odd, perhaps expecting too much from a marriage. But then if I was most women I would have been up to my neck in nappies and shirts by the time I was twenty-one. I certainly would have no interest in the financial broadsheets and matters of business.

"I think she's quite shy from what I gather," I tell Josephine in a way that should convince her I've barely given Constance Armitage any thought. "You generally have one like that in a marriage and one who's more outgoing from what I've noticed. George and I are opposites and I consider it a good thing."

What I really want to say to Josephine is yes, I find it very odd that Lawrie's wife does not stand by his side at work events. I want to say she should see it as her duty, instead of just taking the rewards of being the wife of a successful man without playing her part in the relationship. I would play the part to perfection and more importantly, enjoy every minute of it.

"What does his wife look like?" she asks. Her eyes are glistening with ill-disguised curiosity.

I'd rather not be sitting here with Josephine Briggs pretending to be bosom buddies. Moreover, I'd rather not be made to describe Constance Armitage when the very thought of the woman makes my heart sink and stomach curdle on a regular basis.

But Josephine is waiting for an answer to a simple enough question. I mustn't risk arousing suspicion about the way I feel towards Lawerence. I take my time to choose my words carefully.

"His wife is very petite and dresses smartly," I tell her fussing with the neckline of my blouse.

Josephine is nodding, her silence letting me know she's keen to harvest more information from me. I'm unsure how to elaborate.

"What colour is her hair?" she asks eventually, scooping up the last of her peas and shovelling them between her lips. They're smothered in an orangey-red shade of lipstick; a colour that does not do her any favours.

I'm unable to comprehend the sudden fascination with Lawrence's wife. Perhaps her elusiveness makes her appear intriguing and mysterious. How very exotic to be thought of in such a way. Irritation rises to my chest then my throat, and I try to ingest it.

My mind goes to last Boxing Day when I spotted Constance through the bedroom window. Her face was twisted with horror at being caught peeping out of the very bottom corner in all her glory. Fate meant I just happened to be staring up at that very moment, much to her dismay. That was the reason why she never joined us for tea; how could she possibly face me after what I saw in the fading light of the day?

Josephine's line of questioning is forcing me think too much about Lawrence's wife when I constantly tussle with pushing her to the back of my mind. She knows not what she does.

A split-second decision makes me snatch my magazine and lean forward in my chair.

"It's a shame really," I say quietly now, clutching my magazine to my chest. "Of course, the poor woman hides it well, but she has lost quite a lot of her hair for some reason. I'm afraid she's practically bald in some areas. Lawrence … Mr Armitage, is most concerned about it."

The last part of the exposé was added for good measure. It wouldn't do any harm for Josephine to think I had the confidence of Lawrie, though I've no idea why it would suddenly be so important for me to impress her.

She wipes her mouth quickly on her napkin, smearing her tawdry lipstick in her hurry, and leans into our circle of trust. Our faces lie only inches apart.

"Bald, you say, Daphne, how dreadful. I wonder if this has always been the case."

We remain in our little huddle for some time discussing what could possibly be the root cause of Constance Armitage's troubles. In the end I must dash back to my desk or risk being late for the first time ever.

However, when I tell Lawrie of my predicament only three days later, I could not be more taken aback by his concern for my welfare.

Sadly, by then was it too late for me to stop the rumours tearing around *Lewis's* like a forest fire.

Worse still, it turned out to be too late to prevent the destruction following my peevish moment of indiscretion.

Chapter 12
1918—Constance

Mother hands me my letter and I press it to my heart before skipping upstairs to read it. Later I shall read the words aloud to her but for now the pleasure is all mine.

Leaning my pillow against the iron bedstead I lie back and carefully take the lined paper from the envelope. It has seen better days; this envelope has travelled from France, on a boat across the English Channel, on a train from Dover I think, until Dennis our postman delivered the letter only moments ago. What a remarkable life these little sheets of paper have lived since they left my father's hands a few weeks ago.

In his messy handwriting he doesn't beat about the bush. Within the first paragraph it proclaims he is to come home to us and before Christmas no less!

After almost two long years since he last came home on leave, he is to stride over our threshold and crush me in one of his fiercely protective hugs I love so much. Those hugs are what I've missed the most in his absence.

As I stare at the ceiling, the scene remains incomprehensible, a fantasy which I will only be able to believe when it happens. A bittersweet tear slips down my cheek then my ear to fall on the pillowcase.

The pals he joined up with are all gone. Father didn't write me about those tragedies, it was mother who disclosed the horrifying toll little by little from her own letters.

I shiver, the chill of my bedroom seeping into my dress and cardigan. The fire is unlit and now we are at the end of November the air is damp. Slipping under the bedspread I continue reading father's news—how he looks forward to spending Christmas at home; how he can't wait to see the old tree we put up in the front room flickering away; how he cannot wait for all of us to finally be back together once more. The time for our reunion is nearer still since he wrote the words.

I drag the back of my hand over my eyes in turn. Oh, Daddy, how I've missed you, questioning every single day if I would ever see you again. I still question it.

My bedroom door creaks open, and mother stands with her own letter clutched in her hand. The rare sight of a bright smile lights her face as she stares at me.

"Such wonderful news, Constance," she says, perching herself on the edge of my bed. "But now we have so much to do before daddy's homecoming."

I pull my legs from under the coverlet to sit at her side. She looks smart in her woollen skirt of the deepest green with her rust-coloured blouse and matching cardigan. Mother likes to dress for the seasons; today she is very autumnal.

"What did he have to say?" she asks with a nod to my letter.

As I have done with every other letter father has sent me over the years, I read it aloud and then she does the same with her own. I'm sure father would be horrified that she's so candid, but mother thinks I am old enough now to live in the real world.

I've noticed quite rightly she never discloses the sentiment father signs off his letter with as those words are too personal and for her eyes alone. I often wonder if he uses romantic words to tell her how much he misses her. I suspect he might because living in uncertain times would surely compel you to speak from the heart.

She pats my knee and gets to her feet now, saying, "Well, I think we must put our plans into action without delay," she says. "First and foremost, I would be grateful if you could call at *Glenister's* to increase my Christmas order. I think a goose will be justifiable this year, the smallest one they have available mind. We must place our order today as every other wife who is lucky enough to be expecting her husband home for the festive season will beat us to it. Uncle Seth will contribute his coupons, so we'll have enough funds to indulge just this once."

The thought of us sitting around the table eating a Christmas lunch with all the trimmings, wearing paper hats from crackers spurs me into action. How I took those years for granted before they were taken away from us. In the three Christmases we've spent without him I never dared think about father being at the table with us again.

Mother dashes back downstairs, a woman on a pleasant mission, as I pull my weekend winter coat out of the wardrobe. Twenty minutes past ten says the time and *Glenister's* closes at noon, so that allows me plenty of time to call and see Jennifer in her shop before I join the queue at the butchers.

It's a ten-minute walk to *The Lane.* Mother told me its real name is *Hunslet Road*, so why it's not called *The Road* I've no idea. Most people refer to it as *T'Lane,* but mother is keen to use proper pronunciation. I know there's one or two who think she's stuck up because of this and other behaviours, but she doesn't seem to lose any sleep over it.

What they don't stock in the shops there isn't worth buying, she says, and it's true we rarely need to venture into Leeds.

The fog is curdling with the smoke from the endless rows of chimney pots to create a smoggy atmosphere. I must pull up my scarf around my mouth, losing count of the people I see with the same idea so we can only nod an acknowledgement as we pass. That is until I meet Mrs Pritchard pulling her shopping trolly behind her.

I must tell her about father coming home before she hears it from anyone else.

"Now that's the best news I've heard in a long time, Connie," she says. "You've made my day and no doubt your mother is walking on air. I bet you can't wait to tell our Jenny."

Her daughter, Jennifer, has been my best friend since school. The catholic school was strict, a stickler for etiquette and aptitude but less so for sentiment. It strengthened our bond but more so when Jennifer lost her father to heart failure. That was my first short, sharp introduction to grief as my grandparents had died long before I was born. One moment he was there, larger than life, only to be disappear like a wisp into the ether. Jennifer and her family have lived in my thoughts since father has been away from home.

"That's kind of you to say, Mrs Pritchard," I say, unable to help a note of sadness slipping into my tone. "I'm on my way to run an errand for mother after I pay Jennifer a call."

"Oh, what a Christmas you'll all have," she says, heading off to get about her day. "Say hello to your mother for me."

"I will. So nice to bump into you, it's been a while."

It has been a while; it's not the same since we left school, and I called on the way to meet Jennifer. She waves and I watch her tramp home a moment, her bulging shopping trolley trailing behind her. No more special Christmases for her and her children. Closing my eyes I push away the painful thought before it gets the better of me.

Jenny Wren's is the perfect choice of name for the clothes shop, or perhaps lady's boutique is better, as this is the pet-name of Jennifer's mother.

Jennifer turns and smiles when she hears the chime of the shop doorbell. My nostrils fill with the lovely scent of new things—dresses, bags, shoes—all laid out to entice her more advantaged clientele of Leeds. There isn't one item in the shop I could afford, and neither could Jennifer as things stand, which I think ironic. She took over the premises a year ago using the combined pot of money her mother received from her father's life insurance payout and his death-in-service benefits. It was greater than anticipated and put to good use.

"I didn't expect to see you in this weather, Connie," she says now. "I'm surprised your mother let you out of the house with your weak chest."

"Oh, you know I shinnied down the drainpipe," I say.

We share a giggle before she heads into the back to put the kettle on.

I draw a breath, glad of the barrier of the wall.

"In all seriousness, I've called to tell you my news because I wanted you to be the first to know," I call. "That was until I bumped into your mother on the way here."

She pops her head from behind the curtain, and my stomach tightens.

"Oh? Good news I hope, Connie."

"Yes, it's father, he's …" I swallow madly more than once so Jennifer looks alarmed, "… he's coming home. He'll be back in time for Christmas."

Her face lights up with genuine delight, reminding why she's so dear to me. Our life experiences are shared, the good times and bad. Our only wish is for each other to be happy.

"I couldn't be more thrilled for you and your mother, Connie. I thought something terrible had happened for a minute there."

I needn't have worried so about her reaction, but she would have felt the same in my shoes.

"That's why I'm here, I need to run an errand for mother," I say.

I'm careful not to elaborate and labour the point that we're on track to have a Christmas to remember.

We indulge in two cups of tea, no sugar, using the same tea leaves followed by two custard creams.

We allow ourselves an extra biscuit to celebrate, while Jennifer tells me about her plans to model her new-season dress collection on the pieces on display at *Lewis's* department store. Mrs Mickiewicz can make them at a fraction of the cost so she can sell them as one-off pieces. She's not yet twenty but Jennifer has it all worked out, ensuring she makes the most of the money she's been bequeathed for her family, more than herself. As the eldest she sees it as her responsibility, and I can't help but admire her sheer strength of spirit.

In the end I must dash to join the queue at *Glenister's* before making my way back home. The weather is keeping everyone on Plevna Street indoors. The quietness follows me, so the sound of our front door opening is louder than usual.

I'm startled now by the slam of the door behind Uncle Seth as he bounds into the street.

"Connie, hello, I didn't see you there," he says, his eyes as round as saucers for a second or two until he pulls himself together. "Did you do your mother's bidding and get the goose order in for Christmas Day?"

I'm trying to understand why he appeared so angry when he came out of our house, struggling to find a response to the simple question. Finally, I nod a confirmation as he buttons up his coat, winding his scarf around his neck.

"I've left some oils and canvases old Tom from the pub gave me. His eyesight's going so he can't paint like he could, and I told him you would make good use of them." He pauses so I open my mouth to thank him, clamping it shut when he interrupts. "Good news about your dad," he says.

I don't think I've heard my uncle string so many words together in my entire life.

"Yes, we're excited about it as you will be. I've just been to tell Jennifer."

He's backing away from me, disappearing steadily into the smog as I chatter.

Mrs Baxter is loitering by the window next door, keen to discover what all the noise was about. She gives me a jolly wave, unfazed at being caught in the act of spying on proceedings.

Mrs Baxter may well be disappointed by the anticlimax of a drama that never was. Unlike me, who realises suddenly that not all dramas are a huge kerfuffle. Some are quietly disturbing, much like the look on my uncle's face as he bid a hasty retreat from our house only seconds ago.

Uncle Seth is halfway down the street already as though the devil himself is at his heels.

Chapter 13
1930—Lawrie

"Have you time to join me for a quick snifter at *The Regent*, Lawrie?"

Gregory Coleman is leaning on his umbrella like a walking stick, always the dapper gentleman about town.

We've just finished our Board meeting, and I was all set to head home after a particularly dry run through the quarterly results. My friendship with Gregory has strengthened over the years. Gregory joined the Board three years ago, and it was over drinks following his first meeting that we realised we shared the same curious nature and sense of humour. He can appear a touch too smooth at times and he does like to put on airs and graces to pretend he's from old money but he's an astute businessman with interests in Leeds and London. Most importantly we've always been completely honest with each other …which is invaluable in commerce. He's given me the heads up on more than one occasion that certain manoeuvres from the Lewis family might not in the best interests of the company.

We share another interest too: My wife, or should I say her painting. Gregory considers himself to be the foremost art connoisseur in Leeds and has a gallery, *La Toile,* on Cookridge Street.

'Bringing the elegance and sophistication of the capital to Leeds', the front window brags and it now displays a collection of Constance's work at more than twenty pounds apiece after he spotted the painting she did for my office. His prices are steep, but then with his effortless charm Gregory could sell coal to the coalman. They've become firm friends, and she spends more and more time at the gallery discussing her work and commissions.

"Thanks for the invite, Greg old boy, but I need to take a rain check tonight."

I would prefer to get home as I'm concerned about Constance who seems to have been withdrawing further into her shell recently. I've been building up to a conversation and tonight was the night to broach the subject.

"Oh, go on, Lawrie, one for the road. I have something I'd like to discuss."

His level stare makes me realise there's been plenty of time this afternoon for any discussion we might need in this office, so why not then?

After a second or two of deliberation I decide to telephone Constance and let her know I'll be home a little later. Mrs Osmond assures me she will pass on the message.

Something is wrong, I sense it. Perhaps Gregory is unwell, perish the thought. If it's a business opportunity he'd like to discuss, then we would have done so already.

I don my hat and mackintosh, asking Daphne on the way out to inform Timothy that I'll meet him back here in an hour for the drive home.

The Regent is only a five-minute walk away, the mizzle clearing as I keep pace with my friend. I spot the green-tiled façade of the public house, and once inside Gregory points me in direction of the snug area. This again is most unusual as ordinarily we would take a seat at the bar.

I breathe a sigh when he arrives with our whisky order and sits opposite me on a stool. Raising my glass briefly I take a swig first then watch him intently as he does the same. We're alone, adding to the air of tension and I rush to begin the conversation.

"So, my friend, I can't lie, I'm a little concerned as to why you've dragged me here when Mrs Osmond's steak and kidney pudding is awaiting my arrival," I say attempting a laugh which escapes as a snort.

Gregory glances over his shoulder, and I shiver with a slight quell of alarm.

"The matter is a little thorny to discuss, Lawrie to be honest. I have no time for tittle-tattle much like yourself, but something was brought to my attention which I feel I must broach … as your friend."

Sitting up straight on the backrest I only raise my brows as I wait for him to continue. I'm bemused as to why I should be the topic of anyone else's gossip.

"Well, it's like this: Douglas Woodhouse has told me that he's heard a whisper going about the shop floor."

Scowling, I shake my head. Douglas may be a Board member, but I'm still confused why this should warrant a clandestine meeting and be of such concern to me.

"A whisper; about what? Me? I wonder why I would be of interest when I live a simple life of work and home. I have nothing to offer that would fuel any tittle-tattle."

As I speak, I immediately think of Daphne. Has her secret been discovered, but if so by whom? I'm the only person who knows about the pregnancy and I sense she doesn't care much for fraternising with other members of staff.

Gregory looks as though he would prefer not to have drawn the short straw, his mouth twisting this way and that as he considers his words.

"The gossip is not about you, Lawrie. It's about … it's about Constance," he says, glancing over his shoulder once more.

What? This makes no sense at all, and I'm taken aback. I quickly try to regain my composure in front of my friend.

"I can't think what gossip there would be about Constance," I say as casually as I can muster.

Gregory sits and stares at me long enough however for me to have an increasing sense my simple, fulfilling life is about to shift, and the realisation is not pleasant. True or unfounded, the mud of a rumour has a tendency to stick.

"Well, enough of the cloak and dagger, tell me what nonsense is being spread about my wife. I'm at a loss as to what it could be as she barely leaves the house unless it's to see you."

He holds his hands up saying, "Look, all I know is that there's been mutterings about Constance and a secret she may not have wished to be discovered, not ever … and not publicly."

And then the penny drops, like a cold, hard stone into the very pit of my stomach. So, my place of work is rife with rumours about my wife's unfortunate circumstances. But how could they possibly know? Oh, Constance, I think, should you find out I dread to contemplate your reaction.

Gregory and I exchange a look, but he doesn't push me. I'm grateful because I don't want to say or hear those offending words for fear this would make me party to the terrible gossip now surrounding my poor Constance.

"Have you any idea who started the nasty little rumour?" I ask.

"None whatsoever I'm afraid, Lawrie. I wish I could tell you, but in any case, it won't help the matter.

Greg stares at me as I ponder who the culprit might be. I'm certain he will be wondering if the rumours are true as this is only natural.

Who has visited our house aside from Timothy? I dismiss this notion immediately as he's been nothing but a rock for many a year. I struggle to think who else it might be as we live such a secluded life.

Of course, how foolish of me … Daphne Farrington. I had forgotten about our unexpected guest over the festive season. There isn't anybody else it could be, yet I can't understand how she could have discovered Constance's secret when she didn't even join us that day.

I fight the urge to dash from the pub and back to the office. I should like to challenge Daphne, it must be her who saw something and set tongues wagging, but in my frame of mind this would not be wise at present.

To think how I've been protecting her these last weeks, how I was prepared to help her. Why would she betray my trust in such a malicious way?

But then a familiar saying springs to mind: "Hell hath no fury like a woman scorned." Rightly or wrongly, scorning Daphne Farrington was precisely what I did.

"You know who's at the root of it, don't you?" Gregory asks me now.

Should I tell him I wonder, can I trust him enough?

I conclude that I have nothing to hide or be ashamed of, and I must proceed with this in mind.

So, after I fetch us two more whiskies, I decide to confide in Gregory; the whole tale, exactly as it happened and leaving nothing out. This is not gossip, this is factual, and I do trust him enough. He needn't have told me about the rumour, but he bit the bullet and did it for me and for Constance.

I only omit the part about Daphne's circumstances as I am not a vindictive man. Gregory listens attentively without interruption.

Afterwards I feel cleansed though I was free from any implication in the first place. I'm consoled it was the right decision under the circumstances. It's clear Gregory cares deeply about Constance and I'm grateful to have some support in this on a personal and professional level.

It was well over the anticipated hour when I joined Timothy at the car. He folded his newspaper and greeted me with his usual cheery smile. The familiarity of the scene is welcome after the tumultuous conversation I've just had to endure.

Sometimes Timothy and I chat on the journey home, sometimes I might read the newspaper or some work papers, it all depends, and he knows how to respond accordingly almost as second nature.

Tonight, I sit in silence in the back seat and take out a tiny sheet of paper torn out of the back of Gregory's little black notebook. He handed it to me after he'd scribbled down a name, address, and telephone number and now I stare at the letters and numbers so long they begin to swim around the paper.

Constance will not like the significance of them or indeed what I must do, not one jot. My mouth is dry as I tuck the paper into the inner pocket of my suit jacket and stare from the car window at the moorland.

For my part, I must now remember that when absolutely necessary and when all other avenues have been explored, being cruel to be kind is the only thing to be done in the course of true love.

Chapter 14
1930—Daphne

From the corner of my eye, I see mother is watching me again. Despite my best efforts to ignore her I'm staring straight through the pages of my book. Snapping it shut I slip it onto the low table that sits between us and ask if she would like another cup of tea.

Even this mundane task reminds me of Lawrie and how he takes his own tea—strong and sweet—and I think of him every time as I'm spooning the sugar. There's no escaping him wherever I turn.

A sudden knock at the door has mother and I looking at one another as though something terrible has happened. It has really as our flat is in no state for visitors, but more importantly neither are we. We remain seated as I silently pray whoever it is will go away.

My prayers go unanswered when a second, much louder rap prompts us both into action. Mother plumps the cushions and empties the ashtray while I hurriedly comb my hair and pinch my cheeks in the mirror above the sideboard. There is no time to apply lipstick.

The back of mother disappears into her bedroom as I take a deep breath and reach for the door handle.

His face may be in shadow, but I know immediately who our visitor is by the cut of his suit and his smart brogues. Before my eyes reach his even, I know that Lawrence Armitage is waiting in the entrance of our humble little flat.

"I'm very sorry to intrude Ms Farrington, but I hope you might speak with me a moment," he says, his hat clutched between both palms.

How I've missed his voice, how I've longed to hear it again and now my heart is fluttering like a leaf in a breeze. I realise there was no need to pinch my cheeks for a touch of colour as I'm certain they will be glowing like a red-hot poker.

"Mr Armitage, I apologise but we are not ready to receive guests this afternoon. Perhaps I might telephone you at the office to arrange a more convenient time."

There's a long pause whilst I study the intricate wood carvings of the stair banister.

"Please, I promise I shan't take up too much of your time, but I must speak with you."

Mother will be listening at the door, but this is not the place to have the difficult conversation I know is ahead.

"Is Timothy waiting outside?" I ask.

He shakes his head and if I'm not mistaken, a touch of colour suddenly appears in his own cheeks. I can't imagine how he's travelled here without Timothy and why indeed he should want to.

"I know a tearoom just around the corner where we can … chat. I only need a few moments to tidy myself up and put on my outdoor things. Please, step inside."

As he steps into the room, I think how out of place he looks here in his fine clothes. Our flat is pleasant and homely, but we never have guests of Lawrie's standing.

I dash to find my compact mirror and expertly apply my lipstick in the light of the window. Our eyes catch only for a second in the reflection and I look away, as does he, both I think feeling caught in a strangely intimate act. He stands twisting his hat in his hands and I think too late how it would have been polite to invite him to sit down.

Moments later I'm relieved to be outside on neutral ground as side by side we set off to walk the few hundred yards to the tearoom. My hands are shaking in their cotton gloves as he remarks about the dismal day for the time of year. I can only mutter an agreement, relieved this tortuous journey is a brief one.

"Here it is," I say bringing us to a halt.

He glances upwards at the swinging sign with a small smile, the same smile I had when I first saw *Tea & Sympathy* is the name of the tearoom.

Inside, my eyes roam amongst the steam and cigarette smoke to spot a table by the window and one on the back wall. I decide on the latter; though few people know me in this area, I would prefer us to be in the background. I'm thankful the room is almost filled to capacity as the lively chatter will help to drown out our conversation.

"What will you have?" he asks as I take a seat.

"Only a cup of tea for me please," I say, refusing his offer of anything to eat. I could not possibly swallow a morsel of food.

He orders two teas at the counter, the young waitress blushing as she clatters the cups and saucers.

"I'll bring them over to you, sir," she tells him, all flustered and overcome by his handsome presence. This is par for the course in his world and he only rummages for some loose change in his pocket to pay for the teas. Now he's weaving to join me at the table and my stomach twists tighter with each step as he approaches.

I ran away.

I left my position under a cloud and in a hurry the day Gregory Coleman took Lawrie out unexpectedly for a drink. It was obvious what was happening and to be honest I'd been expecting the grapevine to throw my little grenade to Lawrie much sooner.

I typed a succinct note of resignation, covered my typewriter and abandoned the office I'd worked in for twelve years as though I was leaving for the evening all set to return the following morning. There and then was not the time for histrionics, I had to make certain I was out of the building before Lawrie returned.

Three weeks have since passed and now he's here. Just when I'd managed to console myself that I would never have to face him again yet secretly yearning for him to still be part of my life. It has been as painful as when he went to war, except this time I have shame and remorse to add to the mix. Mother thinks I'm taking some long overdue time off at my employer's insistence as I'm upset about what happened with George.

He unbuttons his mackintosh and places his hat on the table before sitting down in the chair to my right. I'm grateful he didn't sit opposite me, as this at least feels slightly less intrusive and confrontational.

"I apologise again for landing on your doorstep unexpectedly," he says, his eyes on the deep red velvet of the tablecloth. "I certainly didn't plan to come to see you, not today … not ever in fact. It was a spur-of-the-moment decision, and I would not have known what to say on the telephone. I'm still somewhat at a loss, yet here I am regardless."

The waitress arrives with our tea, and we watch her carefully placing the crockery on the table in silence, thanking her in unison as she leaves us.

If there was ever a time to fall at his mercy, it is now.

"I can only apologise for the way I left in such a hurry. I should have stayed to explain," I pause as I feel his eyes on me. "Or rather to apologise."

My throat is knotting as I grab the teapot to pour our tea unceremoniously. I add my own milk and sugar then take a welcome sip from my teacup.

"I admit to feeling a whole raft of emotions since you left, Ms Farrington. To begin with, I was shaken to discover you might be the perpetrator of an ugly and spiteful rumour. I didn't want to believe it, that is until I discovered your note. As you might imagine I have since been annoyed somewhat by your indiscretion as it must be said, it was quite a mean-spirited thing to do, especially when I've done nothing wrong to you. More pertinently, neither has my wife," he adds with emphasis.

I feel like a child being scolded and sit sullenly, accepting of my admonishment. He has every right to say these things to me when they are wholly deserved. I have no defence to offer him.

"However, my intention was not to come here and upset you, I only want to try to understand," he says. "I confess to being surprised by how different it is for me at work since you left. I knew we were a good team, but I hadn't realised how much I relied on you professionally speaking."

Professionally speaking he says, his words sounding terse and cold rather than a compliment. Yet, how can he have missed me in any other way when I was left in no uncertain terms about his feelings towards me?

"I should never have let my disappointment allow me to behave in such a disgraceful manner. I'm still coming to terms with it myself." I force myself to meet his eyes, surprised at the empathy staring back of me. "You're quite right to point out you and your wife did nothing to deserve my spitefulness. I am utterly ashamed of my behaviour."

He leans back in his seat, glancing around the tearoom. Nobody is watching; nobody cares about us and our testing conversation. The world is going on just the same as always.

"Despite my better judgement, I've found myself worried about your circumstances," he says. "I know I shouldn't be concerned by rights, but I can't help myself thinking about your future." He places a hand on the back of his neck and sighs. "Have you told your mother as yet?"

"No, I'm afraid I haven't, though believe me I've wanted to broach the subject many times. I've told her that I'm taking time off work as I'm upset about how things ended with George, I mean Mr Jackson."

He sits quietly with his thoughts a moment before offering me more tea from the teapot, which I decline. He fills his own cup.

"Have you seen him?" he asks.

I did see George only two days ago. In all conscience I couldn't deny him the knowledge that he was to become a father though I wanted to, oh how I did. He deserves to know; I see now it's not his fault that I love another man, a love that meant I kept him in the shadows for years. The poor man did not stand a chance.

"Yes, he knows about the baby and despite everything he intends to step up to his responsibilities though not in the traditional sense."

I'm startled now when Lawrie's hand covers mine, though I don't pull away.

"Can't you marry him? Surely if you can't marry him for yourself, you could do it for..."

I snatch my hand away, so his eyes stretch. How dare he; how dare he tug at my conscience in such a way? As if this decision isn't painful enough for me. My irritation mounts quickly to anger, he has touched a raw nerve and I begin to lose myself.

"Don't you think I would marry him if I could?" I hiss. "I shall never marry him because I cannot live in a marriage where I do not care for my husband, and I'm surprised that you should wish such a thing on me and my child. I am an independent woman through choice as much as necessity. We will be fine, please do not concern yourself. Go home to your wife and child and leave me to my own business."

A hush descends on the tearoom as I realise too late the volume of my voice. Lawrie doesn't appear to notice, but the silence is mercifully brief when people resume their conversations. I suffer the odd glance in our direction from customers only for them to turn away when I catch them in the act.

Snatching my handbag and gloves I get up to leave, stifled by the close proximity of Lawrence now. He dashes behind me trying to keep pace as all eyes follow us out of the tearoom.

I should like to get back to the safety of home and as far away from this man as possible.

"Please, Ms Farrington, Daphne, stop," he says between breaths. "I may never see you again and I don't want to leave things on such a note. I spoke out of turn, but I find myself losing sleep over your future and that of the baby."

I stop walking when I hear those words. The thought of never seeing Lawrie again is taking my breath away as though I'm winded. He is losing sleep unduly over me and I am being callous and unreasonable. Leaning against the iron railings I place a hand to my chest.

"We worked together a long time. I understand now you were far more than an assistant and… and I took you for granted."

I look up to see him staring down at me, a look in his eyes I have never seen before. What can he mean by 'more than an assistant'?

"I mean, I relied on you more than I should have, and I now value the way we complimented each other. I'm a capable man, but you were my stay at work and the person whose opinion I trusted the most.

I never thought you would leave somehow, which is ludicrous when you're quite a young woman. Why wouldn't you leave to start a family? I feel foolish for even thinking it now."

I know now he's not only here because of my professional capabilities. You cannot have someone as part of your life in whatever capacity and for so long and forget they existed. He misses me at work, but I can clearly see he misses me as a person.

"I never wanted to leave because I loved every minute of my job. I made a difference and I felt it. You always took my suggestions seriously, and many were carried through without you taking credit." I stand up to my full height, but I still only reach his collar. "I had a moment of weakness which I now regret. However, I do not regret the outcome for one minute. I always wanted a baby ... I only thought he or she would be the product of a loving marriage."

As we stare at each other in silence, something is different. Our relationship has been altered by our candid exchange; I can sense it.

Fatigue washes over me. I want to get home to mother because I have so much to explain and discuss. It's proving more difficult by the day to hide my condition.

Lawrie extends his hand and I take it though I'm not sure what he means to do. My heart gallops at the thought of him putting my hand to his lips.

Instead, he shakes it twice before letting his hand drop to his side.

"I'm very happy for you in that case. A baby is a blessing whatever the circumstances." A light passes

116

behind his eyes as though he's just remembered something he'd forgotten.

"Goodbye, Daphne," he says suddenly as disappointment sinks my stomach. "I understand now I have no right to turn up out of the blue and interfere in your life."

My name has come from his lips for the first time and the pleasure of it is being pushed aside as I struggle to quash my regret. I thought for one mad, impossible moment the tide had turned.

"Goodbye, Mr Armitage," I whisper.

My thoughts are saturated with sadness as I turn to walk away from the man who captured my heart without knowing and now keeps it under lock and key. I'm unable to look back like the day I walked away from my job, so I can't know if he's watching me still or if he's already heading home to his family.

Back at the flat I close the door and lean against it. How I could crumple in a heap to the floor and sob now but there's no time for that.

Mother is waiting by the door with an odd look in her eye, making me think of Lawrie. Even her stance is peculiar, somehow taller, arms folded in front of her.

"So, it seems I'm a little late to the party, but I realise now you're having a baby with that man," she says.

It's a statement of fact, no hint of a question.

I'm frozen to the spot by the shock of her confrontation and when I don't speak because of it, the look of disgust on her face shrivels me.

She turns from me and walks silently back to the sitting room.

I cry after her, "Mother, you've…" but I stop short when she doesn't turn around, lacking the will and the heart. I'm weary and my sad little world is collapsing on top of me. Convincing my mother that she happens to be wrong in her supposition will just have to wait.

This assumes that I can convince her without proof as she is clearly altered, and I am the one who is guilty of changing her.

Chapter 15
1918—Constance

"Father!" I yell, oblivious for once to the quietness of the street and the noise that will send our neighbours flying to their windows. "Where are you going? Please, come back!"

He continues striding into the darkness so I must increase my speed. My new heels are sinking into the snow, but there was no time to don my boots. I heard the door slam and flew down the stairs from the vantage point where I'd been spying and listening to the commotion.

My father's Christmas homecoming had not gone to plan. I'd allowed my imagination to run riot, expecting him to almost swing me from my feet with joy when he met us at the tram stop.

Mother and I were wearing our Sunday best coats and hats for the occasion, ensuring between us that the house was shining like a new pin before we left. Fancy sandwiches were waiting under brown paper, so preparing them didn't cut into our reunion time when we arrived home. I'd spent the early part of the morning baking father's favourite custard tart with a sprinkling of nutmeg we had from before the war, placing it in the coolest part of the house at the top of the cellar steps. We never made custard tart in his absence I realised then.

Everything was perfect for his homecoming.

Dusk was descending as the tram approached and mother and I exchanged glances brimming with anticipation. The telegram from father had arrived two days beforehand, informing us of his expected time of arrival. We were positively glowing with excitement for the celebrations and festivities that lay ahead, all with my father back with us where he belonged.

He was the third person to alight the tram, meaning he was obscured by another two passengers for a moment. I shifted my head left to right a few times to try to catch a glimpse of father behind them.

Our eyes caught, and I'm ashamed now as I'm sure my expression of disbelief was the first thing he saw. My father was sunken, is the only word I can think of; everything about him, his posture, his frame, even his smile was diminished.

Mother glanced at me briefly, her brow slightly furrowed, and I knew then she was thinking the same. Even so, she was keen to greet her husband, the man who had been taken from her life for almost four years with only a brief interlude.

My mother and father faced each other a second or two, eyes scouring faces, as I heard the tram depart but I didn't turn to watch it. I was transfixed, wondering what would happen between them and waiting for my turn to greet him in equal measure.

Mother pressed her lips to father's cheek and his eyes glistened as he leaned into the comfort of it. His expression was unreadable, neither happy nor sad, but it still somehow spoke to me. I chose then to deny what it might be saying but I've thought of it since.

Finally, he turned his attention to me, his fragment of a smile unconvincing. The hair showing under his hat was duller than I remembered, and his pallor had a colourless tinge about it, so he was almost transparent, ghostlike. Still, I was determined to ignore it all the best I could, raising myself on tiptoes to slide my arms around his neck, pressing my cheek to his.

A wetness appeared between our cheeks. Was it father who was weeping or me?

Mother's voice broke into our reunion.

"Well, let's be having you, Ernest dear," she said, placing her handkerchief in her bag with a snap of the clasp. "Our specially prepared sandwiches will be curling at the edges like a Turkish slipper if we don't get a move on."

We laughed, slightly too loudly edging to the point of hysterical, but it served to unravel the dreadful knot in my stomach. We linked arms, father between mother and I, as we took a steady walk down the two streets to our house. There were neighbourhood friends waiting at the door to welcome father home with the same look of disbelief mother and I had moments before. In between we three made stilted pleasantries about the cold weather, father's journey, the food on order for Christmas. It wasn't quite the reunion I'd pictured lying awake at night.

In the days that followed mother acted as though everything was fine, bustling about her usual Christmas preparations as she was determined to go to town with them this year. Father sat in his chair by the fire at her insistence, pretending to read the paper or a book but I wasn't fooled. His mind was far away from our cosy little parlour.

121

How I wanted to speak to Jennifer about the strange atmosphere our house had been dipped in. I called to see her on Christmas Eve, but too many ladies were still picking the perfect dress or having last-minute alterations. A heartfelt discussion was out of the question.

"I'll call at your house over the holiday to see your father," she told me, wrapping a dress in tissue paper before laying it in the white box with *Jenny Wren's Couture* emblazoned in black on the top. "I can't wait to see him."

It would have been better if I could have warned her of the change in him. Father had barely spoken since he'd set foot in the house. Perhaps though, seeing her sunny little face would be just the tonic he needed.

Uncle Seth joined us for Christmas dinner as planned. He and father had a glass of beer in the house as father said he wasn't bothered for going to the pub.

"Too many people with too many questions," was his excuse and Uncle Seth nodded in agreement.

The whole day was forced, as though we were strangers thrown together for the day rather than family. Uncle Seth went home mid-evening after our cold buffet, and it was a relief to go to bed not long afterwards.

"Shall we take a walk to the foundry?" I asked father as we were having our breakfast on Boxing Day morning.

I was waiting for a rebuttal, but he patted my hand telling me it would be just what he needed after being cooped up for so long.

The streets were livelier than the day before, but still quiet by usual standards as we headed to *The Lane* and beyond. I tucked my arm snugly in his, delighted to be enjoying some time alone with him.

At first, I prattled to fill the silence until I could no longer listen to myself. Arriving at the foundry we stood gazing upwards at the lifeless building that was due to come alive again on the second day of January when the workers would return. The foundry closes for two weeks in August and two weeks in December and has done since I can remember. Over the last couple of years, I have assisted with menial tasks on the floor if they were particularly short-staffed, feeling closer to father than ever on those days. He has worked there his whole working life.

Father took my hand from the crook of his arm, still holding gently onto it as he turned to face me.

"I'm sorry I've been so distant, lass. I don't feel myself is the best way to describe it," he said. "It's been tougher than I thought coming back home. So much has changed since I left, the normality seems a harsh reminder of how many will never return to it."

Our clouds of breath mingled as we stood looking at each other, faces pinched with cold and mutual compassion. Compassion is all I had to offer as I will never be able to understand the full extent of the things that happened to him in France, nor would he want me to.

"Is that the only thing that's bothering you?" I asked, "There…there isn't anything else, is there?"

He flashed me a look, fire in his eyes.

"That's enough surely," he snapped, dropping my hand.

How small I felt at my clumsy choice of words. Of course, that was enough, and I couldn't quite explain it then, but I sensed there was more he wasn't telling me from certain expressions I'd caught. They were less melancholy and more... something incomprehensible. Once he would have known what I meant in asking the question without explanation.

"I'm sorry, father, I didn't mean to offend you. Perhaps we should head home in this freezing weather," I said, turning from him to hastily wipe a tear.

On the way home he asked me questions about work, and all the while I wanted us to address the atmosphere which had swooped suddenly around us.

But I never did.

A whole week of strangeness has passed until tonight and even Jennifer's visit didn't change it for me. She only thought father was adjusting to being home, which of course he is. I must speak to her properly next week once the post-Christmas sale rush has quietened in the shop, I thought when she left.

As tonight is New Year's Eve, I wondered if father would be ready to go to the pub. He could have gone, even if he came home before midnight as he used to do, to see in the new year with us. Uncle Seth tried to persuade him and even mother, but he said he was happy to be by the fire with a drink or two and Uncle Seth admitted defeat. Mother had a stout, and I had a sherry hoping it would warm me and shake the gloom that had been following me around.

The brandy father and Uncle Seth were drinking seemed to be going down rather rapidly. Mother had her eye on matters.

"Whoa, steady on, Ernest," she said, nodding at the bottle. "You'll pay for it in the morning if you're not careful."

Uncle Seth laughed but father shot a look between them both I had never seen before. It was peevish, erring towards nasty. His eyes narrowed, his lips curling briefly over his teeth.

"If a man can't have a drink in his own house after all I've seen and suffered these last years, then it's a poor do, don't you think?"

We all looked between ourselves a moment until Uncle Seth put a hand on father's arm. I gasped when he shook it away.

"Get your hands off me," he spat. "You've been tucked up nicely in your bed while I and too many others have been doing your dirty work."

Uncle Seth jumped to his feet to defend his honour; he was exempt from fighting through no fault of his own due to colour blindness. Father knew this well enough, and he was all too aware how much Uncle Seth had been wracked with guilt about it.

Father squared up to his brother, both drawing themselves to their full height, nostrils flaring. The room was spinning as I gasped for air. Before that moment I had never heard them have a cross word.

"Go to bed, Constance," mother whispered. She nudged me less than gently when I stood glued to the spot, as though my presence was the only thing that would save them from making the next move and going too far with the argument. Perhaps it might have been if drink hadn't been involved.

I took only one step, mother then shooing and pushing me up the stairs before racing back down. I sat then on the top step, grasping my skirt around my calves as I did when I was a child, listening in to mother and father's occasional quarrel.

An ominous silence was interrupted by father.

"Now I come to think of it, *brother*, was it your own bed you were tucked up in I wonder?"

Then came the horrifying sound of expletives and crashing furniture, so after a moment of being riveted, it became impossible for me to just sit there and do nothing any longer. I ran down the stairs but before reaching the bottom father was already bouncing back the front door to stomp into the darkness. I glanced through the open parlour door to see mother picking Uncle Seth up from the floor and bundling him into the fireside chair before I dashed into the street.

I'm now heaving snowflakes into my mouth as much as great gulps of air as I try to catch up to my father. He's yomping down the snowy street, arms marching in time to his feet at almost the speed of a run.

"Father!" I yell once more.

He continues walking as he turns his head to call over his shoulder.

"Connie, go home. I want to be on my own for a while. Just go home."

I stop dead, peering at him with narrowed eyes through the snowflakes. He's getting further and further away from me with each step, his coatless back heading into the distance. He isn't thinking clearly as he's had far more to drink than I've ever known. This is not the behaviour of my father.

When he turns onto *The Lane* and out of sight, a panic forces me to run like the wind, slipping and sliding in the deepening snow.

There are plenty of people milling about despite the weather. Many will be walking between pubs to enjoy the first happy New Year's Eve in nearly five long years.

The last tram is trundling towards us to take the queue of partygoers into Leeds and then it will be a taxi or a long drudge home for them. But the end of the revelling is a long time away, they will be too full of drink by then to care.

Finally, I hurtle past the startled queue of people to catch up with father, reaching out to touch his shoulder before he gets away from me once more. He spins around, his face twisted with fury, so I take a step backwards.

I look down to see his foot slipping from the kerb, stumbling now towards the tram track so my hands cover my gaping mouth. The screams and yells of horrified onlookers seem distant whilst I remain mute, hands cemented in position until I'm clutched face-first into the fur-coated bosom of a stranger.

The commotion going on around me is like a blanket, nothing is coherent, and I should not care if it was. There was nothing to be said that would make it any better and my head is only filled with a barrage of questions:

Would my father have lost his balance if it hadn't been snowing, if he wasn't drunk, if he wasn't furious?

This I now realise I shall never know.

But what I do know is that none of it would have happened if I'd done as he asked me ... and simply left the poor, tormented man alone.

This I now realise I shall live with forever.

Chapter 16
1930—Lawrie

"I wondered where on earth you'd got to Constance, I was beginning to worry."

Slowly, finger by finger she removes her white gloves before carefully placing them on the tabletop. She's deliberately taking her time and making me wait.

The waiter has been hovering, surely thinking I had been stood up until my wife arrived very late and at a somewhat glacial pace. She finally settles down after he graciously tucks her seat under her. Now though she's fiddling and fussing with her already perfect arrangement of cutlery without uttering a word, so I think I might go mad.

To compliment the warm weather, I request our favourite tipple of two large gin and tonics from the waiter. They will serve to cool us down and steady my nerves and if not, I hope the claret I order from the wine list will help with the latter.

Finally, we're left alone but with the table serving as an ocean between us.

"I'm a little late as I've been to see Gregory. I thought it high time he and I had a chat," she says after another long moment.

I regret my need for conversation already.

"Ah, I see. Well then you will have had plenty to discuss. I only hope he reiterated my point that he acted with the best of intentions."

I've been fighting Gregory's corner for weeks now, to little avail. Constance is hurting, and she's been steadfastly ignoring him until today.

"If I'm being perfectly honest, I feel better and worse after speaking with him. He's a dear friend and his support for my artwork is invaluable. However, there's a huge part of me that wishes he'd spoken to me directly about the chattering on the shop floor. He had ample opportunity during our meetings at the gallery."

The waiter arrives with our drinks then stands with his pad and pencil to take our order.

"May I have the sirloin, please and I think the lady will have the chicken breast," I say before taking a long swig of my gin and tonic.

"Actually, the lady will have salmon this evening please," Constance says with a sickly smile.

"Very good, madam," the waiter says, bowing and no doubt wondering what is happening at our table. "May I say an excellent choice, fresh from the Esk only today."

Her smile warms at his comment, or perhaps his approval. We both watch him return to the kitchen.

"Perhaps I was a little presumptuous, but I've only ever known you eat the chicken here," I say, running a finger down the back of my collar.

I take another long drink before puffing out my cheeks. My wife has yet to cast a glance in my direction.

"You were saying that you're feeling better and worse," I say to restart the topic of conversation I rather wish would end.

Her eyes now tilt my way.

"I feel worse, Lawrence, because I know full well who started the horrid rumour. You also know who it is, yet her name has never once been mentioned."

Daphne Farrington is looming large in her absence once more.

"Well, as you pointed out, you knew the person who had been indiscreet, so there seemed no reason to mention the obvious."

My cheeks are blazing so I'm concerned I will appear guilty of a crime I did not commit. Her eyes roam my face, perhaps condemning me already.

"But, my love," she says, the whisper of sarcasm in her tone making me wince, "you had no idea Daphne Farrington saw me through the window that day when she called, so why would you assume I knew who it was. It doesn't make sense that you shouldn't mention her in all these weeks."

Constance has become a little more direct of late. I understand that she's furious with me for discussing her intimate problem with Gregory and yet again I must remind myself I was caught unawares and at the end of my tether.

"There was nobody else it could have been. Daphne was the only person who has been to the house."

I'm beginning to feel ambushed and under interrogation within a crowded restaurant. Now it's my turn to fuss with the cutlery.

I sneak a glance at my wife who looks different, somehow. She appears more…polished, is perhaps the word, as though she's shining a little brighter to the world. Her two-piece costume looks new and will no doubt have been bought at Jennifer's shop. I have a sizeable discount of fifty-per-cent at *Lewis's*, but Constance understandably insists she would feel disloyal if she shopped for her clothes anywhere other than Jennifer's.

Our meal arrives and I'm thankful for the diversion from perspiring under the spotlight.

Her beauty has never been in question—she always shone as bright as the moon to me—but I wonder as I cut into my sirloin if I may have enjoyed having her warm glow all to myself. I swallow the distasteful thought with a lump of steak that sticks at the back of my throat.

"You haven't spoken of *Daphne* much at all over the years. She saw far more of my husband than I, yet she remains this mysterious, enigmatic woman, to me at least."

It's fair to say I did refer to Daphne as Ms Farrington on the odd occasion I mentioned her, but she's reading too much into this. My day may have taken an unexpected turn but when I planned our little soiree, I was looking forward to a change of scenery this evening. The idea was that neutral territory would be the best place for us to have a chat and clear the air. It seems my well-intentioned plans have gone awry.

"There was nothing to say about her. She was a career woman who lived to work, and I happened to notice she had a head for business decisions. We worked well together, but that's as far as it went," I say now.

I keep a level tone though I'm upset we're not making any headway when we've lived in an atmosphere for too long. The evening is going from bad to worse.

She takes a tiny bite of her salmon then sets down her fork, dabbing her mouth with her napkin. I give up and do the same, wanting only to go home.

"I'm sorry," she whispers.

An apology was the last thing I was expecting. Compassion for my wife floods me, so I wish we were alone. Then I could draw her tightly to my chest to try to soothe her weary mind. Instead, I place my hand over hers and hold it firmly in my grasp in the hope of relaying my thoughts. Her lower lip trembles at the gesture, my hand tightening further.

"Shall we go?" I whisper.

There's no need for us to be here suffering in public.

She only nods, so I grab her things and set a hefty wad of banknotes on the table by way of apology for our abrupt disappearance.

It's totally understandable why Constance has been upset. Gregory gave me the details of a reputed psychiatrist when we spoke that night at *The Regent*. We were both more candid than we perhaps intended, and he confided he had been in need of his services in the past. I didn't pry or ask further questions as to the nature of his 'need', but we certainly came to a different understanding in our relationship that night.

I may have thought the conversation with Gregory was difficult, but the one I had with

Constance when I returned home that evening was far more challenging. I was careful to be as tactful as possible, but even so, her secret was flapping madly on the washing line for all to see.

As I hold tightly to my wife's hand on our way from the restaurant, I'm trying to push today's events out of my mind. But it's not to be, they insist on creeping back in as we pass the other couples at their tables, chatting no doubt about their simple little day.

Once upon a time in the not-too-distant past that was us.

Against my will and better judgement my worries about Daphne's plight have not gone away. An unsettling concern for her welfare has driven me to meet with her again recently. It would be nice if others could believe my intentions are honourable, but now a fresh rumour was brought to my attention by Gregory. It threatens my reputation and perhaps even my career if I'm unable to quash it.

Yet how could I find it within me to cast Daphne adrift in her time of trouble? Surely this would make me a cold, hard-hearted man. When she walked away from me the day we spoke at the café, I realised how deeply I care about her as a person. She looked vulnerable when I arrived at her flat; people always seem different at home. You see a slice of their real life, and hers is a very lonely one.

I handled our conversation badly and as she walked away, it was a most disturbing and potentially damaging realisation, however chaste on my part. My sense of responsibility is such that I would not be able to look at myself in the mirror if I was that person who turned my back on someone who needed me.

The *Sword of Damocles* has been hanging over my head for too many months and it may come swinging down at any moment.

If it should, the consequences for everyone in my life will be far-reaching and irrevocable.

So, upon reflection I would only be a fool to let that happen.

Chapter 17
1930—Daphne

The day is far too hot to function properly. I would be struggling with the temperature even if I wasn't in the latter stage of my pregnancy. Every window in the flat is open, but without a breeze the dead heat from outside is oppressive.

I get to my feet in a most ungainly fashion to begin the cycle of closing the windows in turn. From the sitting room I stop mid-task when I spot a familiar head of dark waves. The pleasure is significant, rising from my stomach to my chest to set my heart pounding. The baby shuffles in response then settles themselves once again.

"We have a guest, little one," I say, rolling a hand over my rounded middle with a sense the day has just woken from a slumber.

I always ensure I'm primed and ready for him to appear from nowhere as though he's decided to come on a whim. I only need to powder my nose to dull the glow today. There's nothing I can do about my swollen ankles and tent-like frock, but in any case, he's seen them before. Why I should worry so I have no idea as I may as well be a clothes airer for all the attention he pays to my appearance.

Still, I feel the need regardless.

I open the door. Lawrie is wearing one of his vast collection of light cotton summer suits. He's not really one for the latest trend preferring a more timeless, classic look that befits him better. A bottle of what looks to be lemonade and a small, brown paper bag peep from the top of his open briefcase.

"I thought you might be in need of refreshment on a day such as this," he says, his shy smile like a young boy presenting his mother with a flower.

To think I never expected to see him again. The day at the café had a ring of finality about it and if I'd only had myself to think of, I'm sure I would have sunk into a depression. Mother's accusations about him being the father of my child were of course unfounded, but it took more than my word to convince her.

She paid Lawrence an unexpected visit at *Lewis's* the following day and although she now regrets her rash behaviour, it set tongues wagging, and the damage was done.

Josephine Briggs then called to see me a few days later, just to check how I was after leaving my position in such a hurry. Everyone was worried she said, including herself as I was almost part of the furniture at work. Perhaps her concern was genuine, or perhaps she only came to try to confirm what everyone suspected. For now, Lawrie has managed to defend his reputation but these occasional clandestine, all-be-they innocent visits are dicing with danger for him on a personal and professional level.

I'm constantly reminded that all this unpleasantness could have been avoided if only I hadn't weakened last Christmas.

After visiting Lawrie at home, I was dejected, seeking comfort and solace though sadly I wasn't aware of it at the time. How taken aback George was when, after his father had retired for the evening, his advances were welcomed for once rather than rebuked. Throughout our rather fumbling interlude, George was not at the forefront of my mind. I'm not experienced in such matters, and after the encounter I highly doubt that he is either.

To his credit George was keen to do the decent thing when I told him I was to have a baby. My problems would be tidied nicely away in a drawer if I could settle down with the father of my child. But I just can't do it; with or without Lawrie in the picture it was out of the question for me, and it still is.

After mother discovered my secret I remained at home a few more weeks. In the end though, her snippy comments and inferences weren't good for either of us. Of course I'd let her down, committed the worst sin, and so the situation became impossible.

Hardly surprisingly matters came to a head … over a pan of burned potatoes of all things.

Mother hoisted the pan from the stove and slammed it on the kitchenette worktop with such force it shook the unit, the tins rattling in the cupboard below.

"You, my girl, have been spoiled and overindulged!" she spat. "I ask you, what woman of your age cannot boil a pan of potatoes adequately?"

Enough was enough by then. Spinning her around by the shoulder, her eyes rounded at how near my face was to hers.

"Just in case you may have forgotten, mother, I was busy supporting us after father died. You were happy enough to take my money every Friday if I recall."

She pushed me out of her way with some force yelling, "You should be in your own home with your own man by now cooking *his* tea every night. You've disgraced me; I'm only glad your father isn't alive to see the shame you've brought upon both of us."

The blow was too low to forgive. I snatched my handbag and stormed out of the flat, taking the tram to George's. By the time I arrived, coatless and wet from the spring drizzle, I was a mess, his face telling me as much when he answered the door.

"Daphne, what on earth…" he exclaimed. "Are you alright? Come inside and tell me what's happened to you."

His kindness was too much. I slumped into his arms, sobbing though I knew I did not deserve the comfort from him of all people.

So, that day it was George who returned home with me to convince mother he was the father of our child. He succeeded, but we were misguided in believing this would help salve at least some of her concerns. It only made her wonder why I wouldn't marry George to save face if nothing else.

Any explanation was futile because mother is of a different mindset much the same as everyone else it seems. She will never comprehend why love should be a crucial factor in the equation of marriage.

Pussyfooting around one another then became just as unbearable as her seething resentment, so we mutually admitted defeat.

I'm fortunate my savings will tide me over for a while. I've lived a frugal, some might say tedious home life, especially during the war years and we discovered mother has enough to live comfortably on father's pension.

My new flat is my pride and joy, built in the latest art déco style according to my landlord. So now I can not only cook, but I can clean, launder, iron to perfection and I've been busy feathering my nest in preparation for the arrival of a new baby.

I should have moved out years ago and I might have if it wasn't for the sense of duty I had towards mother and my doomed relationship with George.

These days I can breathe clean air, and I am invisible which suits me perfectly.

Particularly, it must be said, in my current predicament.

I have prepared a backstory just in case I should be asked. I would say I have been recently widowed, and the man who visits is my late husband's best friend. I thought perhaps his brother might be better at first, but then the entwining of a family could complicate the tall story enough to trip me up one day. Friend is a looser, simpler connection.

Now, after I gather plates and tumblers from my sunny, primrose-yellow kitchen I see Lawrie, hands in pocket, staring down onto the street below from my sitting room window. I suddenly have a glimpse into my imagined domestic life together, one that takes my breath away for a moment.

He turns to give me a small smile. The sadness with a touch of pity within it I seek to ignore as best I can.

I continue to live in hope that one day this man might become my family because the hope simply refuses to wither on the vine.

Yet another impromptu visit is surely just another step closer to my dream.

Chapter 18
1930—Constance

I can't deny this dress fits me like a glove, but then it should as Mrs Misckiewicz has tailored it so it might have been custom made. The dress is luxurious in a midnight blue satin with batwing sleeves, a skirt cut on the bias skimming my legs to drape to the floor.

Jennifer rang me yesterday to say it was ready, and all seemed well then. She was reading a letter when I arrived at the shop, hastily refolding the leaves of heavy cream paper and placing them under the counter. Even as she smiled, I sensed her mind was still on the words she'd been reading, but I wasn't going to pry.

I followed her through the curtain into the back room to Mrs Mickiewicz, head bowed at her sewing machine, foot moving rhythmically over the pedal and expert hands sliding what looked like a pale lemon blouse under the needle.

"Ah, Constance, it is very nice to see you," she said, her thick Polish accent giving each word a warm, richness. "I think you will be happy with your new dress."

Her trademark red lipstick adorns her aging lips, and she has a selection of vibrant, silk headscarves she wears tied in a bow at her crown. I've never seen her hair, but Jennifer tells me that at home she wears her silvery-grey waves in a chignon. She retains a glimpse of the beauty she was a young woman.

Jennifer pulled my dress from a long rack of clothes, those which had already been made for the shop floor or altered for a customer. I was eager to try it on like a young girl 'coming out' in London society for the first time. In a way I shall be, though I'm not quite so young and the event is in Leeds. Still, the nervous anticipation will no doubt be the same.

"I never thought I'd tempt you with a dress like this, Connie, but you look beautiful," Jennifer says now.

My cheeks burn at the compliment as I smile coyly. The satin feels cool and almost sensual next to my skin.

"Have you done something different to your hair?" she whispers, though we're alone in the shop.

I beam at her, unable to contain my delight that she's noticed.

"I have a new hairpiece, yes, but I shan't need it much longer." I raise the hairpiece a little to demonstrate my point. "Look, my hair is growing back."

She smooths the shorter strands of hair with her forefinger, her expression leaving me in no doubt about how much she shares my delight. The hair has regrown to almost two inches long already.

"Oh, Connie, I'm so happy for you after all these years. There's no harm in telling you now that I'd almost given up hope of it ever growing back."

I touch her arm, leaning towards her to disclose my secret fear.

"You and me both. I couldn't believe it at first, and of course it took a few weeks to be convinced. But when I first ran my fingers over the downy fuzz that morning, you could have knocked me down with a feather."

"Well, it can take years for your body to recover from trauma, I read about it. I wanted to see if there was anything I could find out to help. Still, it was hardly surprising your hair was falling out after the shock of … of what happened to your father."

She stops talking, knowing she has said too much.

My hand flutters to my neck, and I scurry back into the changing room like a little mouse who had been discovered.

"I'm sorry, Connie, I need to learn when to stop sometimes," she calls through the curtain.

I wipe a tear quickly in the changing cubicle telling her she needn't worry as I carry the memory around with me, regardless. Sadly, I'm only speaking the truth.

"This dress is by far your best design," I call to change the subject. "I can't wait to wear it."

"Have you time for a cup of tea?" she asks when I emerge from the dressing room.

I haven't really, but if I leave now, it will tweak her guilty conscience.

"Of course, I'll make it," I say. "Far be it from me to hold up the workers."

We chuckle together, the air of tension dissipating as I head to the small kitchen area to make three cups of tea like old times.

She's reading the same letter when I reappear but this time, she doesn't hide it from me.

"Any news?" I ask casually. She moves some items so I can place her teacup on the counter. When she looks at me, her lips are in a tight line making my heart sink.

"I'm afraid so, and not good news at that. It's taken the wind from my sails and to be honest and I'm not sure what to do about it."

I knew something was bothering her; Jennifer and I have been friends far too long to pull the wool over each other's eyes.

"It's not Frank is it … or your mother?"

She shakes her head, and I'm relieved at least to know they're both well.

"No, it's nothing like that. It's just I'm thrown because I've had a troubling letter from a solicitor."

Pulling my head back, I frown, shaking my head slightly. This is far from what I expected.

"A solicitor? What on earth is a solicitor contacting you about?"

She hands the letter to me, taking a sip of tea with her eyes still upon me.

Ashford, Bartholomew and Jones it states on the letterhead, and I instantly recognise the name.

"They are insinuating… no, accusing me of copying the clothing designs from *Lewis's*."

If she had slapped me with a glove, I could not be more taken aback.

"Oh, Jenny, you don't think Lawrence has anything to with it, do you?"

Her eyes widen to allay my concerns.

"No, of course not, that thought never occurred to me." Her eyes cloud with tears as she drops her head in her hands. "The problem is that we both know I *have* been copying their designs for many a year. We also know that many of the smaller outfitters and shops in and around Leeds do the same. I just can't understand why I should be singled out of the many."

I place my hand on her shoulder, so unused to my stoic friend getting upset. She's quite right on both counts but it is very odd. My eyes wander back to the officious letter.

"It looks as though they don't intend to pursue the matter further at present," I say, hoping to console her in some way.

"No, though it perturbs me that they've been 'monitoring the situation' for some time. I think at this stage they're only issuing a warning for me to cease and desist." She sighs, her expression when she lifts her head so mournful my throat tightens. "The thing is though, Connie, my reputation will be ruined if this should come to light. It's one thing customers suspecting I undercut *Lewis's* and make a living from it, but it's another thing entirely when they know it. I'm only trying to support my family in any way I can, not swipe their empire from them."

I hand the letter back to her and she reads it yet again as though it might say something different. The underhand nature of the investigations is troubling me too; someone has clearly been visiting the shop incognito for the solicitor to draw such a concrete conclusion.

A slow dawning rises in me as I make sense of the puzzle. The pieces slot together too perfectly as I

146

run through them, so I'm certain who is behind it all and why.

Of course I have no proof as yet, but my intuition is screaming loudly enough for it to be impossible to ignore.

*

I fasten the tiny button on the strap of my new silver shoes and slip a handkerchief and lipstick into my silver-beaded bag. Heaving a sigh of too many emotions I head to the top of the staircase, peeking in Dora's room on the way.

She's pink-cheeked and content in her bed, her mouth slightly open as she sleeps. I've never left her of an evening before and I'd still rather not.

Lawrie is settling his bowtie in the hall mirror as I make my way down the stairs slowly, my dress lifted at knee, so I'd don't trip. My silver shoes twinkle with each step.

His jaw hangs as he turns to watch me, so now I must add self-consciousness to my heady mix of feelings.

"Constance, you look absolutely stunning," he says, his eyes following my every move, so I begin to enjoy the admiration spilling out of them. I have never felt more desirable in my life; my husband is positively eating me with his eyes now and my head spins slightly with the intoxication of it.

"Thank you kindly, sir," I say lightly, a slight quake to my voice. "I must say that you look quite the dapper gentleman yourself."

He does, but then he always does. First thing on a morning, last thing at night and every minute in between he's a feast, waiting for me to devour if I should want. He became 'My Lawrie' many moons ago, but I should have listened to the voice in my ear telling me never to let down my guard, not for one second.

When I finally reach the bottom of the stairs, our eyes meet as though we're seeing each other like the day we met in the chemist. The setting and circumstances could not be more different, yet he has the same effect on me still.

Tonight, I must stand tall and proud beside my husband or risk losing the life we know, the life we had dreamed of in our courtship. I can't … I won't let that happen, not for Dora, not for Lawrie, not for our family.

He wraps my fur stole around my shoulders, stooping to kiss my lips. The kiss is tender until it mounts into something much more, something that makes me tremble. Mrs Osmond's footsteps make us jump apart like teenagers caught kissing by our parents.

"My, you do make a handsome couple," she says, taking in the details of my new ensemble. I must quickly grow used to the attention if I'm to survive this evening; I've lived in the shadows for so long.

Lawrie smiles down at me now, lifting his folded arm at the shoulder.

"Shall we?" he asks as I place my hand in the crook of his arm, my nerves subsiding just a little. He's such a supportive presence.

We bid farewell to Mrs Osmond and head to the car and Timothy.

"Anticipation is all, my love," he says. "Hold that thought until we return."

His raised eyebrows and lazy smile trigger a stirring in the depths of my stomach, one which has been missing for weeks. I've missed our wonderful lovemaking, already wishing the evening away so we can be alone again.

"My, my, look at you two," Gregory Coleman says as we enter the top-floor function room of *John Dysons*. My hand is gripping tighter to Lawrie's arm trying to draw moral support.

As per the usual custom since my secret was revealed, Gregory is unable to stop his eyes straying to my hair. Tonight however, they seemed compelled to scan the rest of me.

Lawrie nudges him playfully with his free hand.

"I am here you know, Coleman," he says good-naturedly.

Gregory at least has the decency to blush, but bats back quick as a flash, "Now, who said that?" He's always unflappable in any situation, much like the old version of Lawrie.

The laugh we share goes some way to calming my nerves. I also indulged in a little 'tonic' at teatime before Lawrie came home to try to settle them; this new world is somewhat overwhelming when I haven't strayed far from home in over a decade. Before then even I lived the life of a church mouse.

We dine, we drink fine champagne and I begin to relax somewhat, even chatting to the Managing

Director, Stephen Tobin's wife, Penelope about my painting.

"She hides her light under a bushel too much does Constance," Gregory says, beaming at me with a touch of pride. "Her paintings are new to the art world but she's gaining a reputation and making quite a splash."

He's sitting opposite us at the table, clearly at home holding court. This life is all he and Lawrie know with their comfortable backgrounds though Gregory grew up in a large, loving family.

"Really?" Penelope asks, "I must visit your gallery soon if that's the case, Mr Coleman."

"At your earliest convenience, Mrs Tobin," he says, her eyes on him, his eyes still on me. "In fact, now Mrs Armitage is venturing into the social world, perhaps I should hold a little evening at the gallery in her honour. What do you think, Lawrie?"

Lawrie glances at me, his strange expression making the smile slide from my face.

"I think Mrs Armitage is very capable of answering for herself," he says, the corners of his mouth lifting now. Gregory only thinks he's joining in with the lightness of the mood around the table.

But I know better.

"Well?" Gregory asks, tilting his head like a devoted puppy as he awaits my response.

I touch Lawrie's thigh gently under the table. I'm not sure if I'm ready for such an auspicious occasion in my honour.

"I think I will give your kind offer some thought, but as you know I'm generally not a social butterfly," adding quickly, "though I think now I may have been missing a trick all this time."

Everyone in my vicinity chuckles including Lawrie, and I have a moment of pride that I, shy Constance Crawford have the wit to amuse such an influential gathering.

Lawrie and I sit chatting at the table with Gregory as our table disappears to dance to the sound of Arthur Sweeting and his many Jazzmen who are uncomfortably nestled like tinned sardines in the far corner of the room. The couples swing and sway around the dancefloor, dazzling in each other's arms as I look on in envy. If I must attend these events more often, I may need to take dance lessons, I think as Lawrie makes his excuses. I watch him head to the men's room and spot many a woman joining me until the double doors swing to a close behind him.

"You look ... well, what can I say Constance, darling?" Gregory says in his usual airy way, returning my thoughts to our conversation.

I have long since forgiven Gregory for interfering in my personal affairs now I understand he was thinking only of my best interests. He has been so kind and thoughtful over the years; we just clicked, and I think of him now as a true friend and not just a business acquaintance. The conversation we had weeks ago was welcome as it cleared the air between us. It also had the effect of bringing me to my senses, so I saw as clear as day that a drastic change to my life was in order.

Seeing a psychiatrist was a step too far, but I compromised by seeing Dr Fitzpatrick and methodically using the lotions and potions he prescribed. I threw myself into painting more, using it as a way to relax and ensured I had more fresh air by taking regular walks on the nearby moorland. Sleep then was welcomed after eluding me for so long which meant I didn't lay awake fretting in the night. My dark worries slowly took a back seat.

However, all these measures alone would not have been enough; I knew I must not encourage hair loss with my constant pulling and tugging in moments of distress. After a few weeks, one method begot the other and less anxiety meant less hair-tugging. I was aware of the problem, but my compulsion meant I was unable to take control of it.

The habit had formed over too many years, but I had to refocus if I was to continue with the life we loved so much. I had to because Daphne Farrington was breathing down my neck and worse, breathing down Lawrie's neck. He's only human after all and giving into temptation is a perfectly human trait.

"I have you to thank in part for looking well. I feel a new woman, especially tonight. Almost liberated if you will."

He stares at me a moment too long before leaning across the table suddenly. It's almost in a conspiratorial fashion, and I must lean towards him in order to hear his voice above the music.

"Constance, darling," he's saying, glancing over his shoulder. "This is awkward for me to broach believe me, as you have become such a dear friend."

"What is it? I ask already uncomfortable. Queasiness washes over me and not just from the glass or two of wine and champagne.

He leans ever closer, so my heart feels as though it's being squeezed in a vice.

"These rumours about Lawrence …" he says finally but doesn't continue.

What is he trying to say? I wait but then I must move the conversation along.

"Unfounded nonsense brought on by jealously I think," I say, hoping to acknowledge the notion but dismiss it instantly. It doesn't feel right talking to Gregory about my marriage in such a way.

My eyes go to the double doors expecting Lawrie to appear any second.

"Yes, but do you know the full measure of it?" he asks, his eyes narrowing and his voice adopting a sombre tone. I'm glad we're the only ones sitting at the table.

"Put it this way," I say, "I know that Daphne Farrington had a baby out of wedlock and there's a heinous lie going around about Lawrie being the father. He insists that he isn't, and I believe him. I know my husband and I know Daphne was obsessed with him for many years. It was quite obvious to me the time or two our paths crossed."

Gregory's eyes stay on me so long his silence begins to make my stomach twist and turn.

Drink has loosened his tongue, and it appears I know nothing. I press a hand to my mouth, the cogs of mind wind whirring and spinning so much they are becoming rampant. I thought I knew everything, but something tells me Gregory is about to enlighten me.

Lawrie catches my attention now though as he weaves his way across the room towards us. Our eyes meld so we may as well be the only two people in the world.

The sensation isn't a pleasant one.

In this moment I have no idea which of us could have the most outraged expression on our face … me or my husband.

Chapter 19
1930—Lawrie

"Hello there, old chap, I wasn't expecting you," Gregory says. "What brings you into the city on this dreary Saturday morning? I thought you'd be nursing a sore head from last night, rather like me."

His voice is a distant echo though he's almost at my shoulder.

I continue to study Constance's painting of the town hall in pouring rain, people milling about the streets in Victorian garb. A horse and carriage have such fine detail I think the painting rather beautiful. I suddenly would hate for anyone else to buy it.

Gregory is waiting for my customary greeting. I must pull myself together.

"Good morning, Gregory, I'm sorry to drop in unannounced, I hope you don't mind. Do you have any private appointments this morning?"

La Toile is the most celebrated art gallery in town right now and Gregory's collection amassed over many years, now including my wife's paintings, are in great demand.

Nodding and checking his fob watch, Gregory informs me he has a client coming at half-past ten. This gives me sufficient time.

I'm unable to predict how this meeting will progress as I'm not quite myself this morning. I left before Dora woke and took the tram, sitting in a café until the gallery opened.

The journey home in the car after the function last night was not the one that I had in mind at the start of the evening. I was expecting there to be a spark of sexual anticipation in the air, both of us desperate to get home; the signs were all there before we left. After bidding farewell to Mrs Osmond before Timothy dropped her home, we would turn to each other, and our eyes would clash, then our lips so we staggered upstairs together and into our bedroom.

I'd pictured me slowly unfastening the zip of Constance's dress, so it fell to the floor. She would loosen my bowtie, unbutton my shirt and press her lips to my chest. I would by then be itching to remove her chemise, so she would lie naked on the bed for me to trail kisses from her neck to her breasts, then her stomach … then below. She would moan when my lips reached the tender part between her legs, pushing my head closer which always produces a groan of pure, unyielding satisfaction. I'd need to discard my suit hurriedly, so I could join her on the bed and love her slowly, gently, eyes never leaving each other until they closed in ecstasy. Her legs would fasten around my waist, so we were locked together as one, moving and whispering words of love until her pleasure was mine and mine hers.

Instead, the end of the evening could not have been more different. I wished Timothy a good evening as I returned to the car in such a tone that he knew not to pursue the conversation further. Constance did the same before sitting she on one side of the rear seat, me on the other, a physical and emotional gulf between us.

On my return from the men's room, the sight of Constance and Gregory engrossed in their cosy chat made me decidedly provoked. I'm well aware they've become far more than business associates over the years, and it never bothered me. From their first meeting they seemed to hit it off as Gregory has such an easy-going way and I think this helped Constance overcome some of her shyness in his company. But lately I've started worrying it's becoming more than that. I'd been seeking to turn a blind eye to the look in Gregory's eyes all evening when he was speaking to my wife. It was not friendly, it was positively lascivious, an insult not only to me, but to her and it was happening right under my nose.

I had no clue what they were whispering about, but the scene was one of intimacy.

I was jealous. Simple, old-fashioned jealousy had taken a hold of me I realised. I found it to be a pernicious emotion, striking like lightening out of the blue, tainting previously innocent acts and situations and banishing all logical thought.

Until last night I had never experienced the vile emotion, but then I was firmly in its grasp, shaking, from anger, from a strange sense of disloyalty when the elusive logical part of me would have known I had no right.

They had clearly waited until I was out of the room before having their little tête-à-tête about what, I can only guess. Perhaps it was how they interacted at the gallery and until last night I was blissfully unaware. My mind was a blur of stirred recollections:

How our relationship had cooled; Gregory's concern for Constance, and in that moment a little green flashbulb went off in my head. By then I was absolutely, unequivocally certain they had become far more than just friends.

Constance was behaving oddly when I returned to her side, her body language telling me something had occurred in my absence. At least, Gregory had the decency to bid a hasty retreat, telling us he had to be up for work in the morning.

I wanted to go home, the pride and happiness I had felt when entering the room only a few hours before, lying in tatters like the discarded napkins strewn across the table.

"Shall we go?" I asked, my tone rather clipped.

She didn't appear to notice, only joining me to do the round of farewells. Endless compliments were directed at my wife by my colleagues and associates saying how much they had enjoyed her company, and how she must attend more future events. She shook hands, and smiled graciously, seemingly unfazed at being in the spotlight. It was the first time I had noticed a difference in her manner in public, her increased confidence, and I wondered if the champagne may have gone to her head. I was annoyed with myself and a little ashamed by then at my irritability when I knew she had only attended the evening for 'us'.

After the excruciating journey home and Mrs Osmond's departure I only wanted to go to bed and put an end to the evening.

However, Constance had other ideas. She flounced into the front room, pulling off her earrings and dropping them on the side table next to her chair before sitting down. She made no attempt to make herself comfortable, perching on the edge of her seat like she wasn't staying long.

I was unable to find the words, and even if I had been able to articulate them adequately, I was unable to speak. I felt out of control, unsure what I would say should I begin the conversation.

"Sit down if you don't mind, please, Lawrence," she said eventually. Her tone was level, yet I still heard the command lacing the request. I sat down, pulling my bowtie to loosen it so it hung to my chest, all the while thinking a conversation at that moment would not be a good idea.

Autumn had made the room chilly without the fire, but Constance didn't seem to feel it even in her thin frock.

"I would very much like to know if there are any more secrets you have yet to disclose to me?" she asked, her eyes chilling me further with their directness.

"Secrets?" I muttered, the cold no longer a concern.

So, that was why she and Gregory were in such deep conversation; he was busy gossiping about me like an old fishwife, taking his opportunity to stab me in the back. I thought we too were friends.

"I would thank you for not insulting my intelligence," she said. "You understand perfectly to what I am referring, and I'd appreciate a frank and honest response."

The Constance before me was in command of the situation and the conversation. Her dress, her hair, thick if expertly applied makeup, in that moment all made her appear a stranger.

The answer she was waiting for would not be one she wanted to hear. I haven't been unfaithful in the truest sense, but I have betrayed her trust. I sighed, my upper body sagging; perhaps it will be a relief to confess my sins, I thought then.

"I assume you're referring to the rumour that I've been to check on the welfare of Daphne Farrington on occasion since she left *Lewis's*."

Her hand went to cover the necklace at her throat. By the look on her face, she wasn't referring to anything in particular. She was quite clearly in the dark.

"You have been seeing her?" she whispered.

My head dropped into my hands at the hurt expression on her face, my bowtie slipping to my lap.

Where have we gone, I thought then; where have the Constance and Lawrie of old disappeared to? We discussed everything once, every matter however small and seemingly insignificant. We were two halves of the same person in the realest, truest sense.

"I have been seeing her, but certainly not in the way I'm sure you imagine. Please, Constance, she was a loyal assistant who has found herself alone in the most challenging of situations. I can't find it in me to turn my back on her and … and desert her. I can't be that man."

My voice cracked on the last word, knowing how pitiful my excuse sounded even to me.

"Do I have to remind you, that woman took great pains in ruining my reputation and then yours, that she is still trying to make your position untenable at work. Now, I have discovered third hand no less, you are still seeing her behind my back. I completely and utterly believed you when you denied you are the father of her child. Now though, Lawrence, I have no idea what to believe."

The remark stung like a resounding slap to my face. Did I really expect her to believe I only wanted to help an old friend in need? I had no business being jealous of her relationship with Gregory when I was guilty of far worse.

"Constance, you are the only woman I have ever loved, believe me. What I've been doing was wrong, and I knew it, I know it, but my sense of loyalty is strong, overpowering sometimes. It's one of the reasons you grew to love me, you told me as much."

She leaned forward in her chair, tears sparkling her eyes so I could hardly bear it.

"Don't you see, my love, you have contradicted yourself. Loyalty has only one face; you cannot be loyal to two people simultaneously or the loyalty is null and void."

I stretched out my hand to take hers, but she jumped up from her chair and dashed out of the room as quickly as she entered. There was no opportunity to offer any consolation or compassion and I sat most of the night in the chair thinking of her upstairs, alone and weeping. She didn't answer when I knocked, and the lock was turned so I slunk back downstairs.

Now, I'm sitting in the chair of Gregory Coleman's office and enough small talk has passed between us for an uneasiness to have descended on the quiet room.

I know what I must ask of him today and I can only hope that he is in agreement: I must ask that he *never* discloses the full extent of my secret.

The one which will surely destroy my marriage once and for all.

Chapter 20
1930—Daphne

I see him before he sees me. He's taking great strides across the deserted parkland whilst I use the cover of the ancient oak tree to shelter from the perishing weather. November is not a time to be taking a brisk walk in the park with a two-month-old baby. He's wrapped up well though against the damp air and I tuck the blue woollen blanket mother crocheted further under Hector's chin. As I raise my head to await our reunion, a slightly woozy sensation makes the park scene seem as though it's underwater for a second or two.

His face is a frozen mask, his warm breath disappearing over his shoulder as he walks towards us. I enjoy watching him approach though I wonder what might be in store for us when his eyes lower as spots me.

I thought it rather odd he asked to meet me here. The telephone call was brief and to the point, like a verbal telegram relaying precise and succinct instructions where to meet. There was no enquiring after Hector's wellbeing even. He has been to see him only once since he was born when he paid a brief visit to my flat.

"Hello, you look positively frozen," he says now, glancing inside the perambulator at Hector. "I apologise, I didn't stop to think how cold it would be. Shall we go to the tearoom to get warm?"

I considered leaving Hector with mother, but I didn't want to arouse any suspicion with her as things are going well with regard to our relationship.

"Perhaps that might be wise," I say.

There isn't a soul around as we begin the walk of a few hundred yards to the tearoom.

"It's surely the coldest day of the year," I say inanely.

He nods, humouring me with a distracted half-smile.

We take only a few more steps before he stops walking and turns to me making me come to a sudden halt alongside him. I engage the brake of the perambulator with the toe of my boot as a force of habit.

"What is it?" I ask, reaching out a hand to touch his arm. I think better of it.

Every muscle of his face sags, his eye becoming glassy so I think he might break down. This time I place a hand on his forearm, and he doesn't snatch it away. It rests there quietly I hope conveying so much in the absence of words.

"Daphne, tell me truthfully, have I ever led you on in any way or given you false hope?"

My answer is resounding and immediate.

"No, never, I can assure you of that at least, if that's what's bothering you."

His mere existence is all that gives me hope. His actions and words have never been anything other than that of a colleague and perhaps since no more than a tepid friend.

"You know, I had no idea how much I valued you as a person until you stopped working alongside me every day. I equate it to how I feel about Timothy, although because you're a woman and I'm a man, society insists it must be different for us. You were a solid constant in the background like he is, dedicated and dependable."

I recoil at the last choice of words. Shame forces me to drop my hand and lower my head to look at the frostbitten gravel of the path at our feet.

"I know how ashamed you are of your behaviour, but I've come to understand why you were driven to do it. You were thwarted and alone, jealous no doubt. I've had a taste of it with my wife recently and I assure you it did not sit well. I'm ashamed of how it made me feel and behave now."

I whip my head to look up at me, thrown by his confession but also his understanding.

"I was deluded and saw signs that were never there. You're quite right, bitterness and jealousy consumed me and … and I constantly berate myself for it."

Hector mews in his perambulator and we both stoop instinctively to look at him. I'm thankful of the distraction of stroking his cheek so he settles. He's snug and warm whilst I suddenly begin to shiver.

"Shall we go to the tearoom?" Lawrence asks again.

I cannot think of anything I'd rather do less in this moment.

"No thank you, I must get home. Hector will need feeding soon."

I'm sure he would like to explain further, but I'm painfully aware of the connotations surrounding this meeting. I'd prefer not to listen to any of it, or I might make an embarrassing spectacle of myself in his presence yet again.

His eyes are on my son, his face soft and tender like a father might look at his own son. I close my eyes briefly, irritated with myself. Yet again I'm seeing something that isn't true. Any person looks at a tiny, helpless baby in such a way, be it their parent or otherwise.

"I wish I could turn back the clock and have been open and honest with Constance after our first discussion last Christmas Eve," he says. "We might all be in a different place now if I had. But I didn't want to hurt either of you, it's as simple as that. Now though my hand has been forced and I hope that if you're unable to forgive me, you might at least understand."

So, there we have it; our visits are to be curtailed. Lawrence will never again be part of my life or Hector's on any terms. I knew we were skating on thin ice but now it has cracked, and I have been plunged into the freezing water, the weeds of our secrets and lies binding me so I can have no hope of swimming to safety.

Yet, I forgive him already. His pain is my pain; my love will force me to release him even against my will.

"You must return to work," I say, calmly like the former *Ms Daphne Farrington, Assistant to the Manager of Lewis's Department Store* as it used to state at the bottom of our official letters of business.

I feel far from that woman now.

"Remember, you do not owe me anything, not even an explanation, but I appreciate you meeting me face to face, nonetheless. Please, do not distress yourself any longer, Hector and I will be fine. We are not your responsibility. His father is making provision for us more than adequately and we haven't yet ruled out the possibility of him seeing more of Hector if I choose to secure part-time employment.

Hope ignites then diminishes immediately in his eyes. I can never return to *Lewis's* and my old position even if I was bold enough to face the scandal.

Lawrence leans over the perambulator to touch Hector's cheek so gently with his gloved hand that I doubt he felt it.

"Thank you for your understanding," he says, dully. The words reach inside me to squeeze my heart with an icy hand.

We stand in such close proximity I'm able to study every muscle and line of his face in profile as he stares at my son. I allow my eyes to roam freely because this is the last time I shall ever see the wonder of it.

If I was candid enough to tell him, I may have one last parting gift.

Mother is unaware, as George is even as I registered the birth myself. After much deliberation I chose to record George's name as the father on Hector's birth certificate. It was preferable to the alternative of 'Father Unknown' though it does allow him certain rights. Regardless, whatever his thoughts may be on the subject, the record cannot be changed.

Would Lawrence be touched or horrified that I took it upon myself to give Hector his name as a middle name? Perhaps he would only be indifferent. I only know I consider Hector Lawrence Jackson to be a noble, upstanding name, boding well for my son's future.

As a warm tear rolls down my cold face, I wipe it away hastily, so Lawrence doesn't see. I make my decision: He may understand why I chose his name, but the knowledge will not make a blind bit of difference to *my* future. It will not encourage him to continue seeing me and my son from time to time, each visit keeping me going until the next.

The night times will now become a source of dread to stretch out ever longer and ever lonelier.

I have a lifetime to get used to them.

Chapter 21
1919—Constance

Watery afternoon sunshine fills the backyard, drawing me outside. The wind hits me as I open the door, so I fasten my coat to it and pull up my collar. I'm not ready to be out in public, but the walls of the house are coming in on me. This little spot is presently my only chance of solitude.

    The aroma of Mrs Baxter's cooking greets me as I perch on the bench by the kitchen window, but it does nothing to coax my appetite. Food and mealtimes loom as I sit under mother's watchful eye.

    She's only hanging up our laundered clothes, so it won't be long until she's back downstairs wondering where I am. I'm still absent from work on compassionate leave, but I'm eager to get back to the foundry and next week I shall return whatever mother says. The woeful expressions and words of condolence will be over and done with, and I can then try to move onward to the next part of the grieving process. Whatever it is; however bad it is, there's only one alternative, and that is to put my head down and get through it. Sooner will be better.

    I lift my face to the sunlight and close my eyes, deep breaths making my chest heave. I mustn't cry again, not today. Jennifer called earlier, and we had a little weep in the kitchen out of mother's earshot. I've yet to see mother cry though her complexion is pale and drawn and she's rather withdrawn and dependent which is not like her. I am not like me, so it shouldn't surprise me.

"I had no idea how bad the pain is, Jenny," I said, my wet cheek on her shoulder, "I hope I was there for you when you lost your father. I can't help torturing myself that I wasn't enough support for you."

Her hold tightened around my back.

"How could you possibly know what it's like, Connie, and you've always been a dear friend to me. In any case, the circumstances are far worse for you. Stop that silly talk now or you'll make yourself ill."

I mustered a tight smile as we drew apart.

"It's not a competition, you know, there aren't any winners here."

Her lips tilted, and she rubbed my arm briefly before putting the kettle on the hob yet again. If I drink any more tea, I'll drown in it, I thought, but one after another they're set down in front of me, abandoned when possible or swallowed down with encouragement without tasting a single drop.

"Constance, where have you got to?" mother calls now.

The devil appears at my shoulder whispering to sneak out of the back gate and face the consequences of disappearing from home unannounced afterwards. But then I'll only have to field pitying looks or uncomfortable questioning from well-meaning neighbours.

Resigned to my fate I open the door to step back inside my cell.

"Ah, there you are. You'll catch your death of cold out there if you're not careful."

Her tone is warm and kindly making tears sting my eyes as I hang up my coat. This snug kitchen was once my sense of home.

"Your Uncle Seth is calling but he won't be staying for tea tonight. He bobbed his head in a minute ago on his way home from work to get changed.

Uncle Seth ... why is he paying us an impromptu visit? I haven't seen him since the funeral and was relieved not to have to face him alone. It was a blur of a day that I can barely remember.

Mother still has no idea I heard the bitter end of their conversation that night. I'm convinced it will forever more feel like it happened yesterday, and I've been unable to stop myself replaying the last words Uncle Seth and father spoke to each other.

I run upstairs to splash my face with cold water and sit on the floor with my back to the door, uncaring of the freezing floor tiles. The click and slam of the front door in the silence announces my uncle's arrival after a while; he never knocks or uses the back door as father did. Indignation makes me grow hot and dizzy and I wait longer than usual to respond when mother summons me.

Uncle Seth is standing as mother sits in her chair by the fire. He looks a little less at home than usual, his shirt buttoned to the top with a tie, covered by a sleeveless jersey I've never seen before. In the past he would sit reading the paper for hours or occasionally smoke a pipe by the fire until mother complained about the yellowing of her net curtains.

A sketch pad and a tray of water colours lay in wait for me on the table under the window. He will have needed to make a special trip to *Rafferty's*, the art supplies shop in Leeds, as these are too specialised for them to be found on *The Lane*. Once the gesture would have flooded me with endearment.

"Hello, Connie," he says, "I hope you're … managing." He struggled to find the right word, before nodding to his gifts. "I thought those might help to cheer you up."

He's speaking to me differently. I wonder if this is because I've just buried my father—his only brother—or if he knows I overheard their disagreement only moments before he died.

"Thank you," I mutter politely, finding it impossible to say more.

He gestures with his hand to the chair for me to sit down. I would prefer not to hear what he clearly has come to say but mother turns to look at me now, her eyes narrowed.

"Constance, your uncle has come to speak with us if you would do us the courtesy of sitting down."

I shuffle the few steps towards the fire and sit opposite her, the heat from the fire increasing my flustered state of mind.

He begins to pace behind us, pulling on his lower lip. My uncle is a man of few words; not caring for books or politics or anything else father enjoyed, so they have always been like chalk and cheese.

I happened to love Uncle Seth's quiet nature once; I found it somehow comforting.

"Just tell her, Seth and be done with it," she says quietly after a second or two of watching him. "She isn't a child any longer, she wasn't a child before all this happened."

Her tone is encouraging rather than admonishing. I grip the chair arms as though I might slump to the floor. 'This' does not come close to describing the scale of the tragedy and the after-effects.

"Well, there's no easy way for me to say it, Connie, but I'm moving away," he says, still pacing. "It was different when your grandmother was alive, but she's been gone for a long time now and I need a fresh start. I hope you don't think I'm deserting you and your mother at such a time, but I think it might be for the best."

Mother is staring at my uncle, tears brimming her eyes, but I'm unsure what they mean. Is she sad that he's leaving or upset about how difficult it is for him to tell me. I try not to think about the fact she has yet to shed a tear for my father.

I discover the answer, my throat so tight now it's paining me.

She loves him; my mother loves my uncle. And the look on her face tells me that it's a deep and powerful love, one not appropriate for a brother-in-law.

"Yes, I think it for the best," I whisper, the words still managing to fire and hit the targets like seven bullets.

They both turn together to stare at me. Mother's wounded gaze turns to one of suspicion, whereas Uncle Seth quickly looks at the floor.

"And why on earth would you say that, Constance?" she asks, her eyes still misted, a note of irritation in her voice.

The look she's offering swings me back to being the obedient daughter, one who would never question my parents, only bowing to their authority. I turn my face to the fire taking quiet deep breaths to soothe me.

"I meant because it must be difficult for Uncle Seth to continue living here without father. Perhaps sometimes it's better to turn away from pain rather than stay and suffer."

She nods after a moment seeming placated enough. She glances now at my uncle with a sad smile and their eyes meet briefly.

Of course, I would never deign to point out to her that it will be awkward now father has gone for my uncle to be visiting us every day. It was a different time during the war, normal life was suspended, but now tongues will wag, and mother would not like that at all.

Itss not long before Uncle Seth announces he must be going, saying he will call and say goodbye before he leaves in a week or so. Apparently, his plans to escape Hunslet were set in motion shortly after the funeral.

Mother sees him to the door, and they exchange a quiet word or two out of earshot before she returns to the room. Her composure appears to be restored, and she settles down with her crochet. We barely exchange two words for the rest of the evening, eating our tea in silence.

As I lay in bed, I recall the events earlier and mother's expression when Uncle Seth told me he was moving away. I twirl my hair round and round my forefinger, the repetitive action soothing me. For the first time since father died, I do not weep. Instead, I stare at the ceiling, father's last words to his brother prevalent in my thoughts, spinning and turning on a loop. I wonder if his brother does the same each night.

My hair is a little thinner of late, though it's barely noticeable except to me, and I've been wondering if perhaps it's a result of the shock of witnessing father's death. Jennifer's mother told me once about a woman who received such sudden and terrible news about her son's death that her hair turned white overnight. Perhaps this is similar.

As I pull my hand away from my head, two single strands of my fair hair sit between my forefinger and my middle finger, and I stare at them a moment. I feel nothing, realising my hair is the least of my worries.

I return to work the following week as I hoped, and mother agreed it would do me good to get out of the four walls.

It's just awful approaching the foundry on the first morning remembering one of my last conversations with father, an unpleasant one at that. I make sure to arrive early and head to the toilets to compose myself. I'm in two minds whether to go home before anyone else arrives, but it will only need to be faced tomorrow, and then it will be harder still.

My colleagues in the typing pool wish me good morning but nobody mentions the elephant in the room, not even to say that they're sorry and I'm grateful. I set about my work, making the odd comment to try to lighten the strained atmosphere. The afternoon is better and then eventually enough days go by so it's almost as if my heartbreak never happened, for them at least. When they get their coats on at the end of the working day, I envy them going home to have tea with their families without a care in the world.

Over four months pass before mother finally notices the bald spot that I've taken great pains to disguise. She sees it when I'm coming home from work, turning around to close the door to shut out the wind.

The look of horror on her face makes my hand fly to my scalp to pat my hair back into place. But it's too late.

"Constance, your hair!" she exclaims.

Mother has always been so proud of my hair and my appearance in general. She's been known to boast about me at times to the point where I've felt awkward listening to her.

She hauled me to see Dr Fitzgerald at the next available appointment, and another and each time I tagged along obediently. Then came the wonder of the day I met you, Lawrence, a beaming light in the darkness.

When my uncle left without fuss to go to his new life in Manchester, mother gradually withdrew further into her shell. She had little to distract her day to day and we become two people sharing a house while living in two separate worlds in our minds.

I really should have been more upset about what was happening to my hair, but I was lost in a dense fog of despair which stretched as far as I could see. I could almost reach my hand out to touch it.

I think I saw it as my penance.

Chapter 22
1930—Lawrie

I stand next to Penelope Tobin, both of us studying my wife's latest work in great detail.

Constance has been painting prolifically of late and I suspect it will be serving a dual purpose for her: She can lose herself in her work whilst at the same time avoid spending time with me.

In contrast, she's spending more of her time than ever with Dora. Often, when I bob my head around the door on returning home, our daughter is playing in the room at the end of the hallway we have dedicated to her mother's art. It's a beautiful room overlooking the rear garden, conducive to allowing the artistic juices to flow, Constance said when she chose it. How excited she was to have a room of her own to spend time doing the one thing she has always loved the most. Sometimes Dora will be working on her own drawing at the tiny easel we bought her one birthday. It can be a few moments before either of them is aware of my presence. I watch them and study their facial expressions at work, both so different in appearance and nature, yet so bonded.

"Your wife is indeed very talented, Mr Armitage," Penelope says now. "I'm rather ashamed to admit that I thought Mr Coleman might be humouring her." She leans her head towards me, "I hope this can be our little secret."

I think Gregory may well have been humouring Constance to begin with. I thought he was doing us a favour, but her work has slowly grown in popularity even though she has never had any formal tuition in her life.

"Of course," I assure Penelope, "I often think I have a favourite, then I discover her next piece. What is it you like about her work?"

"I'm no expert, but I think perhaps the fact you say she is self-taught gives her work a prosaic quality. Take this alleyway scene for instance, there's fine detail in some areas and not in others, so it appears somewhat soulful and charming rather than contrived." She chortles to herself. "Listen to me, I sound like a pompous old art buff. My only yardstick for choosing art for my home is that it whispers something to me when I look at it."

I smile down at her. Penelope is very easy company, and she never flirts with me, so this puts me at ease in her presence. I wish I could say the same at work. Three temps have come and gone since Daphne left. I'm unable to find anyone to even match her calibre as a secretary, never mind an assistant. One even thought she could work her charms on me so the whole situation became insufferably unprofessional. I never had time for such nonsense, but now more than ever I'm painfully aware I'm walking on quicksand with the tawdry rumours about my personal life.

"What are you two in cahoots about?" Constance chides, breaking into my thoughts.

I slide quickly away from Penelope who looks rather taken aback. A constant sense of contrition follows me everywhere nowadays, so I appear guilty of something all the time.

Penelope recovers first. "I was just saying to your husband that this painting will sit very nicely in my home. You have made a sale, my dear, assuming it is still available, of course."

Constance beams, clapping her hands together so Penelope and I exchange glances, revelling in her delight.

She's positively twinkling beneath the bright lighting of Gregory's art gallery, her deep red dress a demonstration of her growing confidence in social situations.

"What am I missing?" Gregory asks, striding over to stand by Constance's side. Her excitement is infectious, and they share a smile.

Something stirs in the pit of my stomach; I quickly admonish myself, only too pleased at her success when she has waited a long time to make a ripple in the snobbish world of art.

"Mrs Tobin would like to purchase *Still Alley*, Gregory, how wonderful is that?"

He nods his approval at Penelope saying now, "Truly wonderful—that makes it our third sale of the evening…so far."

"Third? I just can't believe it, Gregory. Here was I worried I might suffer the humiliation of not making a single sale," Constance says, reaching out to touch his forearm. The scene is one of shared empathy, intimacy yet again and I suffer a wave of rejection as they walk away with Penelope to secure the sale.

"It looks like I will need to be quick off the mark in future if I see a piece I resonate with, Mrs Armitage," Penelope says. "Perhaps you might consider giving me first refusal for a time as we have our new apartment in London to adorn."

As the group disappears from view, I turn to face *Still Alley* again with a galling realisation. This evening is my cast-iron confirmation that my wife and I have grown apart.

I would very much like to go home which has become a recurring thought, but it will seem like sour grapes if I do. People will think I'm resentful of my wife's success when this couldn't be further from the truth. I only want to share her moment in the sun with her, to experience the joy together, nothing more. She has been my unwavering support for many years; I couldn't be prouder.

So instead, I make my way to a cubicle in the men's room, but even as I rest my forehead on the ice-cold metal of the door my feverish thoughts are in no way eased. I lose any notion of time passing until the outer door opens.

There's a shuffling of feet then Gregory's voice calls, "Lawrie, is that you in there? I wondered where you'd got to."

I flush the chain to allay his suspicion as to why I would be hiding in the men's room on a night when my wife is receiving well-deserved recognition.

"You look white as a sheet, Lawrie. Are you alright?" he asks, as I appear from the cubicle.

"Sorry, Gregory, I think I may have eaten something that didn't agree with me at lunchtime. I'm trying my best not to spoil Constance's big night."

I concentrate on lathering my hands with soap and avoid Gregory's gaze through the mirror. Drying them on one of the pristine white towels stacked on the shelf I throw it into the basket provided. Everything about the gallery is classy, but then it needs to be.

And Gregory Coleman is a classy man … a classy, personable man who just so happens to be unmarried. The archetypal eligible bachelor.

I stand up straight and make eye contact, facing him head on. Neither of us look away for more than a few seconds and I can only hear the drip of the tap in the basin.

"If you don't mind me saying so, you haven't been yourself for quite some time, Lawrie with all the furore at work," he says finally. "I promised to keep your secret and that still stands." He stares at me still. "Have you seen anything of Daphne Farrington recently?"

I'm astonished then irritated by his candidness. I hoped never to discuss the matter again.

"No, I haven't seen her for some time. Why would you ask such a thing?"

"I'm sorry, I only want to help. You're becoming more distant by the day," he says.

I spin around to face him, and he takes a step backwards.

"Has Constance mentioned anything to you?" I pause, my suspicion mounting. "I hope you don't think you can use this information against me to allow you to get my wife on side."

His eyes widen then flood with annoyance.

182

"I would be very careful about your insinuations, Lawrence if I were you. My reputation is clean as a whistle, and I certainly do not prey on other men's wives … especially when I consider that man to be a trusted colleague and *friend*."

His response weakens my position, pride suddenly rearing its head, so my resentment seeks to make me lose control. This is not me; I am not this man.

"Must I keep defending myself," I proclaim, ignoring the fact that Gregory hasn't even raised the subject. "There is and never has been anything other than a friendship with Ms Farrington. I care … cared about her first and foremost in a professional capacity, as you do my wife, then as a person who has been part of my life for many years, again, as is the case with my wife. However, I severed all ties with Ms Farrington even before it was brought to my attention that she reported Jennifer Pritchard's shall we say debatable business decision-making to the Board."

Gregory shakes his head, saying now, "I see you are in the midst of grave marital difficulties and things do not appear to be what they were. Your little bird is spreading her wings and I for one, perhaps a little selfishly, hope this may continue. I might only suggest that you accept the change before it becomes too late … for you."

His words cut me to the quick, so a shiver runs down my back. He has foretold in no uncertain terms only what has been preying on my mind for many a month. It may already be too late.

A knock on the door startles both of us.

"Gregory, Lawrie, are you in there? Is something wrong?"

We size each other up a moment longer until I exit the room ahead of Gregory to see Constance hovering by the door. Her beautiful face is pinched with concern, so I would like to take her hand and escort her home to sit by the fireside and chat about the success of the evening over a nightcap.

But the night is young, and I must sit through it knowing my wish can never come true. Those days are gone seeming less likely to return with each passing day.

I have no clue how I can restore her faith in me; our sweet, uncomplicated love story has been spoiled and it can never be the same.

The worst of it all is the knowledge that I have nobody to blame but myself.

Chapter 23
1930—Daphne

I close the door behind me silently and creep on tiptoe into the sitting room. Hector has become a little clingy of late which means that despite mother's protestations that I'm spoiling him, I've taken to rocking him to sleep in my arms before placing him in his cot.

His eyes often jolt open as he's lowered but today, so far at least, my efforts have been successful.

"You've made a rod for own back there if you ask me," mother told me, so now I refrain from discussing the problem with her. It will pass I know, and then I'll be longing for the days when he never wanted to leave my side.

A rap at the door makes me stop in my tracks and wait with one ear cocked to see if Hector stirs. All remains quiet and I breathe a sigh.

Whenever I have a caller other than mother who lets herself in with a spare key, I always wonder if they might be Lawrie. The thought flutters in my ribcage. Weeks have passed since I saw him last. Perhaps he may have had a change of heart.

I dismiss the thought as quickly as it came, scolding myself for allowing my thoughts to run away with me yet again.

A brief glance pacifies me the room is presentable enough to open the door.

The gloom of the landing means my eyes need a second to adjust, but when my eyes eventually settle on the person standing there in their glamorous attire, I fight the urge to slam the door shut and lean against it, gasping for breath. I grip the doorhandle, the shock making it impossible to raise a polite smile even.

"Good afternoon, Ms Farrington. I apologise for calling unannounced," Constance Armitage says. "I hope you might spare me only a moment of your time."

My mind casts back to the day I landed on her doorstep unannounced.

I would like to use the excuse of a sleeping baby who can often be awoken by the drop of a pin; that the flat is a mess; that I'm going out even. But I'm too intrigued by her visit and in any case, a guest must be made to feel welcome, unexpected or otherwise.

"Certainly, please, do come in," I say in an unfamiliar voice.

Once inside she waits for me to close the door and lead the way. It's obvious where we are heading as my flat is beautiful but compact, not enough room to swing a cat let alone raise a baby, as my mother pointed out when she first saw it. Still, the fire is blazing, and the tiny Christmas tree is twinkling away cheerily in the window. I'm proud of my home and this will be my first Christmas I can enjoy it.

"May I offer you some tea ... if you have time?" I ask, praying the answer will be the one I wish to hear.

"Thank you, but no, I must call into town for some last-minute gifts before I return home. I shan't intrude on your day for long."

She follows me to the fireplace, and I extend my hand to the chair opposite mine. She looks different and not just because her hair is a little darker which suits her. I can tell it's her own hair because of the texture. It seems she has conquered her problem, and her slight air of confidence will have plenty to do with it. She moves and acts like a woman, when before she always seemed rather girlish, though I haven't been in her company for years.

My own appearance has taken a back seat of late. I suddenly feel very frumpy in my woollen dress, fit for the snowy weather, but not exuding glamour.

She carefully and elegantly removes her gloves and places them on the coffee table next to her handbag of what looks to be the softest leather. I imagine all the items will be from the latest *Lewis's* range, along with the coat she removes which I hang on the coatrack by the door. I slide my hand down the expensive wool before ambling over to sit down. I'm certainly in no hurry to join her.

"Your home is very cosy," she says with genuine admiration.

"Thank you, I do like it here," I say, wondering how she discovered my address. Perhaps she asked Lawrie or contacted his latest secretary. I have no idea and it would be rude to ask.

"Well, I suspect you may know why I'm here. It has taken a great deal of courage to come today, and I wouldn't have done so if … if a dear friend of mine wasn't in need of my help."

My cheeks burn as my eyes drop to the new hearthrug I bought recently. A little treat to myself to finish off my Christmas decorating scheme.

"I'm not entirely sure to what you are referring," I say, swallowing my discomfort. I'm not certain why she's here as it could be one of a number of reasons.

"Please, Ms Farrington, I implore you to do the decent thing and admit to your part in the worrying predicament to which my friend, Jennifer Pritchard, finds herself."

So, she's not here to challenge me about starting the rumour about her hair loss, or indeed about seeing her husband behind her back. I'm sure she would not be happy for her husband to liaise on a personal basis with another woman, let alone one who had tainted her reputation.

"I have no idea what you mean," I say, "I've never heard of the name Jennifer Pritchard..."

She raises her hand, so I stop talking.

"You are quite right to adopt the moral high ground. My friend is all too aware she should not have done what she did even though many have done so before her, and I'm sure still are. There are far more distinguished establishments than *Lewis's*. However, I did not only come here to discuss my friend's wrongdoings however insignificant they may be in the grand scheme of things."

I press my hands tightly together on my lap, bracing myself.

"Why then are you here?" I ask after an uncomfortable moment.

She sighs and reaches for her handbag, scrabbling inside until she finds a cotton handkerchief with C.E.A initials in the corner. She hurriedly dabs a tear before the blackness of her mascara drips to spoil her skirt. I'm at a loss to think of any suitable words of comfort; I have many secrets from this woman. As I watch her, I admit to having an odd feeling I have never encountered before.

"I apologise, I had no intention of crying on your shoulder," she says now. "I came here today as I've been pushed to breaking point on behalf of my best friend, but also because I'm tired, Ms Farrington." She loses her composure a second or two, so her face crumples and she pushes it into her handkerchief. "I'm tired of trying to stay one step ahead wondering what ploy you will come up with next to upset me; of thinking you might want to entice my husband away like I have since before he was my husband even. In short, I'm exhausted of thinking about you. I just want us to be left alone to try to rescue our marriage. I know now that I will never be able to do it without you constantly at the forefront of my mind."

Despite my best intentions, her words resonate with me, and I recognise the feeling I had as one of empathy. I assumed I was the only one suffering, in my case the pain of unrequited love, yet all along she has been suffering just as much for different reasons. We have lived in each other's minds for too many years, I realise. I found it easier to demonise *the girl*, as I always thought of her, it made it better to justify my behaviour. In my eyes she was the winner—she had Lawrie's unwavering love—so I was the loser in the equation.

Yet, all this time she has been obsessing over me in the same vein. I've given her plenty of just cause, certainly over this last year, but as her husband pointed out, this woman has never done anything wrong to me.

It's not her fault that her husband loves her as he does, that they have a beautiful home and daughter. She didn't do this to spite me, she was only living her life whilst I festered with resentment because of it.

Jumping up from my seat to stoke the fire I think I might cry too. My eyes lower to look at her, a tear settling in the outer corner of my top lashes though it only sits there.

"Will you answer me one question?" she asks.

I immediately know what it will be, it's the same question I have been called upon to answer before to my mother.

I nod, backing away to return to my chair.

She sniffs, looking like the young girl I remember on the day they told me of their engagement. The day that changed my life forever and led us to this moment.

"Is my husband the father of your son?" she asks, her green eyes rimmed with redness, her bottom lip trembling.

She delivers the words with a thick coating of pain. Oh, to be in a position to have to ask such a dreadful question. How many months has she sat with it at the back of her throat to almost choke her?

If I tell a lie, I know it will be the end of them and if that's the case, then perhaps there would be hope for Lawrie and me. My heart takes flight then plummets like a kite that has lost the wind behind it, so it crashes to the ground. How foolish to think for one second that he would want me if I could be so callous, and to his wife at that.

Regardless, why would I want to do such a thing to a man I love? A shudder runs to my very core at the thought of what I have become to even contemplate it.

This time more than ever before, I must be convincing when I answer the question.

"No, absolutely not, your husband is not the father of my child, you must believe me. His name is George Jackson, and we were to be married. Your husband is in love with *you*, and he always has been. His duty towards me is not at all any kind of love."

I hold her eyes for a moment to try to convince her until I can stand it no longer and drop my head in my hands. The pain I can see, the pain I have caused is too much.

"I'm grateful for your honesty," she says after a while. "I'm sorry, I must look a terrible mess."

She takes her mirror from her handbag and wipes her face with her handkerchief. Her beautiful face is swollen and darkened from mascara like a bruised peach as she wipes her cheeks then powders her nose.

"May I ask you a favour?" she says as she drops her compact in her handbag. "It's not a small one by any means and of course you must reserve the right to refuse."

My shoulders tense in preparation, then I hear what will be the first of no doubt many cries from Hector now he's awoken alone in the room, his mother nowhere in sight.

"Please excuse me a moment," I say, with a small smile. "My son is calling me, and I assure you he will not stop until I answer."

Hector is bawling and flailing his hands as he lays in his crib at the foot of my bed when I rush in. He stops crying as soon as he sees me, showing me that I am his world, as he is mine.

Today has taught me that I've wasted too much precious time already in his young life by longing for something that is out of my reach. My son has a mother, a father and a grandmother who love him and should be a significant part of his life. They want to be, and they should be, as so many children are not fortunate enough to have a family at all.

Drawing him into my arms I lay my chin on his head as his arms slide around my neck. His baby scent grounds me as I close my eyes and whisper soothing words into his hair a moment.

Sighing, I know I have delayed long enough; I must return to the sitting room to face Constance and hear her request. I owe her that much at least.

I leave our bedroom with Hector still in my arms and glance at an empty chair; Constance is nowhere to be seen. I wonder if she might be in the powder room until I spot her coat has disappeared along with her handbag and gloves.

I stare at the indent of the cushion, hoping to prove to myself she had been here to visit, that it wasn't my imagination, then spot a small piece of creased paper waiting on the coffee table. Picking it up it seems it was once her shopping list which has been scribbled out. I read something, 'doll' at the end of a line not entirely blackened with ink which I assume must be a Christmas gift for Dora. Perhaps there will be other items listed for Lawrie that I shall never know about.

I sit with Hector still clinging to me, his face in my neck, and read the couple of sentences written in swirling italics on the rear side of the paper. The formation of the letters is far from perfect as she will have needed to write in a hurry. I imagine her grabbing her outdoor things to rush out of the door afterwards.

As I ponder the implications of her request it dawns on me now that I had no idea when we shared our sad little smile only moments ago, it might be the last time I will ever set eyes on the lovely Mrs Constance Armitage … or indeed her husband.

Chapter 24
1931—Constance

Gregory's office is proving a welcome retreat from the month of January.

I'm cosseted in the warmth and the silence of the room, occasionally interrupted only by the tinkling of fine porcelain cups and saucers. Only the best for Gregory in every respect.

When he told me he would like to exhibit my work I thought he was joking to begin with until he convinced me it could be a lucrative business proposal. I had more than a flicker of pride knowing I was gifted enough in his discerning opinion to be on display in the houses of the great and the good of Leeds. Even Londoners have taken to paying him a visit, combining their trip to Leeds with the taking of the waters in Harrogate and surveying the medieval architecture of York. The gallery has established a reputation of note.

"So, that makes seventeen pieces in total sales, Constance," he says, looking up from the ledger on his desk. "It's a mighty good job you had a backlog of your work in storage, or I doubt we would have kept up with demand. Ironically, clients will now have to wait or commission your work which will benefit us greatly."

Locking his hands behind his head he sits back in his chair, calling for Mrs Fisher to come in with our tea when she knocks. She's a more mature lady he employs on a part-time basis as he sees fit, generally when clients are expected. As she only lives a stride away, she can be called on at a moment's notice the rest of the time. Retirement is not on her agenda. Her husband has passed away and the days are long, she told me. I'm certain she's older than mother yet she looks a good deal younger.

"There you are Mrs Armitage," she says setting down the tray before me. "I saved the last of the Christmas shortbread for you as I know they're your favourite.

Her conspiratorial wink makes me smile warmly at her as I lay the tea strainer on the cup.

"*Her* favourite, what about me, Mrs Fisher?" Gregory teases. "It's me who pays your wages after all. You would do well not to forget that."

She sniffs and flounces out of the room but not before she's thrown him an impish little grin.

I love it here for many reasons, not least of all Gregory's easy manner. It's become a home from home over the years.

I'm relieved the festivities are over. I've tried my best for Dora's sake, but having Lawrie at home was testing. When he's at work and I'm painting or when I'm here, I can almost pretend all the drama of last year never happened. His presence is a stark reminder.

"How was your Christmas?" Gregory asks now.

Such a perfectly natural question, a cliché we all ask one another after the festivities but today the banal words affect me.

"Oh, fine," I say, reaching for a shortbread. I put it to my lips then realise I'm not at all hungry, replacing it on my saucer with a small sigh.

He rises from his chair to spread the tails of his suit jacket and perch on the edge of his desk only two feet away from me.

"Is everything alright, Constance?" he asks quietly.

I tilt my eyes his way then find myself unable to hold his gaze.

"You know it's not," I say flatly, my cup tinkling gently in the cradle of the saucer.

How I feel about my business associate has become blurred and out of focus. We've always shared an affinity, but I have a conflict of my heart unsure if my fondness of him is friendly, or something more.

I was disappointed with Lawrie when he discussed my secret with Gregory behind my back. The issue was compounded by him knowing for certain about my hair loss, rather than just courting a rumour. It was then I began to wonder why I should care so much about Gregory's opinion of me in terms of my attractiveness as a woman.

"Of course, I'm aware you and Lawrie have been weathering a blip in your relationship," he pulls his cuffs further down his arm one by one for his gold cufflinks to peep under his suit sleeves, "but this happens in a marriage. You have been together a decade, so how can one expect to sail through married life when one is constantly changing?"

I take a gulp of tea and set the cup and saucer down on the tray to give him my full attention.

"Quite the matrimonial expert, Mr Coleman, I see," I say, unable to disguise a hint of playfulness in my tone.

His sigh is quiet.

"Few people know this, but it will surprise you to know I *do* have some experience in this area."

This comment makes me sit up quite literally and take notice. Gregory has never offered even a crumb about his romantic life.

"Are you saying you have experience of marriage?" I ask.

His expression darkens, and I curse my curiosity for making me push the matter.

"I was married as a young man once, yes. She … my wife left me, and I vowed that day I would never remarry. I wanted children, and she didn't, sadly, a conversation we neglected to have until it was too late. One should never assume; I can testify to that."

His vulnerability makes my heart go out to him. I've never heard him speak in such a way before and I'm quite honoured he felt he could confide in me.

"I'm so sorry to hear that, Gregory, it must have been a very difficult time for you."

"I haven't spoken of it in so long, I'm surprised I have today. An old wound has been opened I thought was healed many years ago. You seem to have a knack of cracking my shell, Constance."

Our eyes meet, fear of missing the opportunity propelling me to take a chance.

"If I'm being honest, Gregory, I feel the same." I pause briefly, my heart beating too fast, "I have started to wonder why this might be."

We continue to stare at each other, the tension hanging between us so now neither of us can ignore it and carry on without addressing the turn of events. I'm unable to look at anything but him, the walls coming in on me as I'm left with an uncomfortable disadvantage. The ball is now in his court.

He clears his throat, and my eyes follow him as sits down in his chair on the other side of his desk. In a matter of seconds, I have altered our course, and I would like very much to retreat to safety.

"Constance, for what it's worth, I think you are understandably a very unhappy woman at present. Yet, I have no doubt you love your husband despite your misplaced feelings."

My face falls into my hands with shame. I have no romantic inclinations towards Gregory, nor he I, I knew it even before it had to be pointed out to me. A terrible lapse of judgment has now put our friendship and our professional connection at risk.

Oh, I must face it head on, I have lost my mind.

I sit forlornly with my cheek in my hand and stare at the fire, wondering how I have arrived at this place.

Eventually I turn my head to see Gregory crouching at my feet, his expression one of concern.

"Please forgive me," I say quietly. "This behaviour is so out of character, and I only hope you will seek to look past it."

His warm hand covering mine on my lap makes guilt wrench my stomach. I'm not deserving of such compassion after my deplorable conduct.

"I have been looking past it these last months, knowing how you are floundering. But you have a husband who would die for you, Constance. I think you may have been so burdened by bitterness you have forgotten." His eyes roam my face. "I have seen a change in you but also in him because he believes you love me whilst you believe he loves Daphne Farrington; it appears you have much to discuss. I only know I am not the answer to your troubles, my dear."

My free hand falls on top of his, catching and ensnaring our deep connection with one another. My friend has reminded me whom I love, have always loved despite our difficulties.

I would like to ask Gregory if there is anyone he loves or even cares for, but now is not the time. I only hope he doesn't live a lonely life.

If he wasn't the perfect gentleman, he might have taken advantage of my vulnerability to lead me down a dark path with a dead end … and no hope of return.

Chapter 25
1931—Lawrie

The house stands silent. No sounds of supper being made, of Dora's playful chatter and the other domestic noises I take for granted. My stomach immediately ties itself in knots at the ominous void, a sense of dread taking hold of me.

I'm reminded of the time I walked into the house and found Constance in a terrible state. Since then, I've lived in fear of my world slipping through my fingers in one way or another.

I hang up my coat and loosen my tie, dropping my briefcase on the seat of the telephone table.

Grasping the sitting room door handle I hold on to it a few seconds before heaving air through my nostrils and opening it. The unknown is lying in wait on the other side of this door; I fear it.

Constance is sitting by the blazing fire under the light of the standard lamp behind her. Her stockinged legs are crossed, and she holds a drink in her hand. She's wearing a pale green woollen suit I've never seen before I assume she purchased from *Jenny Wren's*. If I were an artist like my wife, I would like to paint this perfect still life of homeliness to remember always. This was not what I was expecting to walk into, and relief is a comfort.

She turns her face to look at me, her smile filled with such sadness my throat catches. I'd like to run to her side, but I know we must talk to each other, communicate; nothing more, nothing less. She is clearly of the same mind and so my stomach begins to settle slightly.

I remove my suit jacket and tie, dropping them both carelessly on the sideboard so the vase rattles but stays in place. I would not care at this moment if it shattered into a million pieces, nothing shall deter me from my mission. As I head over to my chair, I roll up my sleeves and notice a tumbler of whisky waiting on the side table, the ice cubes still perfectly formed.

She has been planning this moment. A flicker of hope ignites inside me for the first time in months.

Constance appears the epitome of self-assurance, the only sign of nerves is her foot twitching rhythmically in midair as it dangles elegantly from her crossed legs. How endearing it is to see it; nervousness means she still cares.

She reaches over and waits for me to join my glass with hers, the celebratory tinkling putting me further at ease. Neither of us say the customary, "Cheers," our eyes only melt together before I take a long swig of my finest whisky. We haven't made eye contact since we went in the car to the soiree at *Dysons* I recall suddenly. Oh, how I've missed the solidity of it.

Without food since lunchtime, the alcohol hurtles around my bloodstream, so the room appears woolly around the edges for a second. It hits the spot perfectly and I settle into my seat with a small sigh.

Her head tilts as she studies me, perhaps noticing the dark shadows under my eyes and grey pallor for the first time. I've seen them staring back at me in the bathroom mirror, but if she sees them, she doesn't pass comment.

I wonder what brought her to this moment on this particular day when yesterday or weeks ago would have been better. I quash the thought; the here and now is all that matters. If now is the right time, now is soon enough.

"Where's Dora tonight?" I ask.

"Mother has taken her out for afternoon tea to Leeds at my request. I asked her to take a taxi, but she insisted on taking the tram as an adventure for Dora. She packed her little vanity case as she's staying over at mother's this evening."

So, we have the house to ourselves. This is a first and ordinarily would be quite a treat, except now I strangely feel as though I have lost the protection of Dora being in the house.

Constance takes a drink as I watch her, savouring the effort she's made for me with her appearance. It's almost as though she's planned to seduce me.

"You look beautiful," I tell her.

She gives a wry smile saying, "Oh, this old thing, I've had it months if only you took the time to notice."

Once this was our little joke, but tonight the words are a stiff and stilted. We must stand on ceremony for the time being as we're out of practice.

"Lawrie," she says, at precisely the same time I say her name. Our laughter joins, the joyous sound of it relaxing my shoulders.

"Ladies first," I say.

"Lawrie, I have so much to say and so much I need if not want to hear from you," she pauses, placing her glass down. "However, this conversation must be totally and utterly honest. If anymore, shall we say untruths or withholding of information ensues to spare each other's feelings, it will surely be the end of us." Her cheeks are flushed. "Are we in agreement?"

I have nowhere to turn. It's a fair request, yet telling the truth or not, either way risks it being the end of us. My wife has me pinned firmly against the wall with her hand at my throat.

"*Do* we agree, Lawrie?" she asks again, the brittleness of her tone coercing me to nod without hesitation. It would not be wise to close the door or even alter the course of this conversation.

She reaches to take a sip of her gin and tonic before entwining her hands on her lap. She's most definitely in charge of the discussion this evening.

"I have a story to tell you, one which I should have told you long ago. Forgive me."

Her face turns to the fire as I sit and wait for the tale to begin.

*

How could I have prepared myself for what was to come with that simple opening prelude? The words threw a veil over the horror story that unfolded line by line to churn and twist my insides.

She told me of the tragedy of her father's death. She said the words calmly, matter-of-factly almost as though she was reading from a book so for a while, I was unable to comprehend the extent of what she was telling me.

As she spoke my heart raced faster, then it began to pound as though I was frantically running to keep up with her.

It proved impossible.

That terrible burden she has hidden from me was pouring from her, swirling like a torrent to get to the end of the confession as quickly as possible. As the words sank in, I understood why the torment she lived through manifested itself with physical symptoms. The burden has been steadily corroding her confidence, her sanity, her entire life, resulting in where we were before she clawed her way back.

Now, I have only added myself to the list of people who have betrayed her trust: Her mother, her uncle … now me. The guilt tightens my chest, a tear falling near my lips, so I wipe it away quickly with my palm. Constance fails to notice as her eyes are still fixed on the fire, doggedly pursuing the end of the tale so she can be free of it once and for all.

That she should hide it from me is unthinkable. I could have helped her, made her see it from a different perspective. Surely this is what my role is as her husband.

The only person who was her stay was her father, and he was taken from her in a way that would haunt a person forever. The death of the man who was 'more than a father' as she once described him to me, has left her with blood on her hands. This is what happened in her own eyes if nobody else's.

I close the gap between us and sit at her feet, grasping her hands.

"Constance, stop, please. You talk as if you're to blame in running after your father when it's the most natural thing in the world to do. I would have done the same myself, anyone would. You must see reason don't you see, or you will never be able to make sense of it."

Slowly she drags her eyes from the fire to look my way, the rawness staring me in the face searing my heart. A strangled sob escapes me, the noise startling as much to me as Constance, I have never cried in front of anyone before. Even when I lost my father, I cried behind closed doors.

Her arms encircle me, her head on my shoulder and I drop my head onto her lap, wetting her skirt with my tears. Despite everything we are one person, the horror of my wife's trauma becoming my undoing.

The guilt drives my sobs into almost a wail, putting an end to our conversation like the snuff of a candle.

I now know that when, as per our agreement, I'm forced eventually to tell her the ending to my own story, I will be the culprit of adding to her already insurmountable pain.

Chapter 26
1931—Constance

Mrs Baxter is at her open bedroom window pegging out the washing when I arrive at mother's house to collect Dora. The washing line ends under the window of number twenty-five on the opposite side of the cobbled road and her sheets are already swinging in the breeze.

"You're hopeful," I call, nodding to the wet pillowcases waiting in her hand. "It was raining when I left home."

"This wind will lighten them at least," she says, glancing at the sky. "I haven't seen you in a while, Connie."

She's quite right, she hasn't because I generally avoid coming here if I can help it. The house, the street, they never change, and though this is often the definition of home, for me it only stirs too many memories.

"Dora slept over last night, so I'll see what she and mother have been up to. Nice to see you, Mrs Baxter," I say with a wave.

Smiling down at me, she returns the compliment and resumes her task, the schedule of her day and her week written in stone like mother's. On it will go until it inevitably ceases one day in the future.

As predicted, Dora is hanging the washing on the clothes pulley over the kitchen fire when I arrive.

Mother's sleeves are rolled up, and she's putting the washtub away on the cellar head. They both greet me at the same time, Dora leaving her post to slide her arms around my legs.

"Mummy, I'm helping grandma with her washing like I help Mrs Osmond sometimes," she says, her face aglow like it's the most exciting task in the world. Her hair is falling from her bun, the wisps framing her face. I trace my finger down her pink cheek.

"So, I see and what a good job you're doing between you," I say, ignoring mother's look of disdain. It tells me I should not allow my daughter to be involved in menial jobs when we employ a housekeeper. She has passed comment about it before, but I choose to ignore her.

"Let's finish here and I'll pop the kettle on," mother says, helping Dora hang the washing in a poker-straight line on the airer. Standing side by side they look at ease with each other, working in tandem. Mother nods and smiles her approval at Dora who beams with pride.

"I'll put it on, you two look very busy," I say, taking off my things before fetching the kettle from the hob. Mother finally relented and replaced her coal-fired range cooker last year, being one of the last on the street to do so I imagine. The kitchen is repainted in the same dirge green colour each spring and the wallpaper in the rest of the house remains the same as when I lived here. Mother doesn't believe in unnecessary frippery and expense, but the house is always spotless.

"You've done a lovely job, Dora. I think as a special treat you may call at the corner shop while your mother and I make the tea," mother tells her, folding down her cuffs.

She heads into the parlour and returns with a shilling coin, pressing it into Dora's palm.

"Ask Mrs Dobson for three iced fingers, and then you can treat yourself to a quarter of barley twists. I know they're your favourite sweeties, and you've been a big help to your old grandma this morning."

Dora thanks her grandmother with bright eyes and my heart flutters with something. Perhaps a touch of envy that I've never felt at ease with mother the way Dora appears to. If I were to mention it to mother, heaven forbid, she would tell me I was imagining things or that it's different with grandchildren.

The back door closes, and I watch Dora from the window as she opens the gate, imagining her skipping down the ginnel to the shop, her heart full of the giddiness of buying childhood sweets.

"So, did you and Lawrie have a pleasant evening?" mother asks, scooping the tea leaves into the teapot.

Perhaps I'm reading too much into it but something about her tone makes me wonder if she knows more than I would like. Has Lawrie continued to disclose too much on his ad hoc visits I wonder now.

"Yes, it made a welcome change. Thank you for having Dora," I say, leaning my shoulder against the cellar door. I make sure to avert my eyes as I know they're rather puffy from a long sleepless night.

Mother sets the tea tray as I study her. She looks up suddenly, startling me by shining a spotlight in my eyes when I wasn't expecting it.

"It was a pleasure, and I should have done it sooner," she says, sugar bowl in hand. I'm squirming under her gaze and wait for her to resume her task, but she doesn't.

"Is something wrong?" I ask.

"Well, as you should ask, I sent Dora to the shop so we might have a moment of privacy," she says. "I've been dillydallying long enough, and I thought it high time I took the opportunity to speak to you alone this morning."

My heart sinks knowing she's about to interfere in matters that do not concern her once again.

"Constance, it's long overdue that I told you as you mother that you must pull yourself together ... before you're too late."

Her knuckles gripping the handle of the sugar bowl glow white. This conversation is difficult for her at least.

"I must speak up though I'm well aware your marriage is no business of mine. However, if you choose to ignore me, you're at risk of losing the love of a good man. I would be shirking my duty as your mother if I turned a blind eye to the situation any longer."

After delivering her thoughts on the matter she bustles quickly into the parlour. The kitchen linoleum tiles swim beneath me from the shock of her words. I take some time to slow my breath, the dizziness subsiding enough eventually for me to follow her.

"What has Lawrence been saying to you?" I ask. The question comes out more like a demand.

I sit at the table under the window, the room darkening with rain clouds. The glow of the coal fire should make a warm, cosy atmosphere but I'm left cold at the thought of the conversation afoot.

"Lawrence? He has said nothing whatsoever to me," she says, hands on hips. "I have eyes and I can see the change in you both."

Today of all days I don't feel up to speaking about our business. I'm drained and wrung out from the confessions of last night, but my mother is not a patient woman.

"You've seen a change in *both* of us, but I'm upset you see it as my fault alone that we are having difficulties. Of course, 'Lawrence the Golden Boy' would never do anything wrong, he could never put a foot out of line."

I make an attempt at humour, but it falls short, only sounding sarcastic.

"I only know you have always allowed your nerves to get the better of you since you were a young girl. As you will remember, he discussed his concerns with me before Dora was born and to my mind things have become worse. A man will not put up with a wife who is floundering forever, nor should he. If you can't pull yourself together for Lawrence, then you must do it for Dora."

Twice now she has told me to pull myself together; after last night she has caught me at the wrong moment to bow to her authority for once. I get to my feet to tower over my mother. She knows absolutely nothing of our relationship and particularly my husband's lapse of judgement. I assume there will never have been any mention of this.

"I have allowed my nerves to get the better of me, you say, mother. I wonder why this might be."

I ignore her startled expression; the train has departed from the station and will not stop until it arrives at its destination, not today. Her inference has pushed me to the edge of reason. My chin tilts upwards, years of pent-up resentment suddenly making me bold.

I have things to say, it shall be now or never. Perhaps her timing is perfect after all.

"You know nothing of what has happened between Lawrie and me but just to be clear, mother, I will not be taking advice from a wife who betrayed her husband. Who not only betrayed her husband, but with his own brother no less. People in glass houses should not throw stones, not if they have good sense."

Her mouth gapes, her eyes growing almost to the size of the saucers lying untouched on the tea tray.

"Yes, it's true, I know all about your inappropriate relationship with my uncle. Father did too; if he hadn't been so upset by it, he would never have stormed out of the house and … and he would still be here with me now. I told Lawrie about it only last night. The time had come because as you say our marriage is in crisis. He was very distressed as one would imagine when I have withheld this from him for so many years. However, he's right about one thing: I did not contribute to the death of my father because *you* did, you and my uncle."

I hold on to the chair back. "Yet, you have the gall to tell me I will lose the love of a good man if I don't pull my socks up!"

She stumbles to her left, almost collapsing onto the settee as though I've shot her. I stand firm, blood pounding in my ears. My whole life I have never lost my temper in such a way and right at this moment, my mother's obvious distress does nothing to affect me.

I can only hear the hiss of the coal fire and the endless ticking of the mantle clock as she sits in a stupor.

"Constance, please, let me get this straight, do you mean to say you have been living with this cloud since you were a young woman; that most of your … behaviours and conditions were brought about because of it?"

I take two steps backwards to return to my seat at the table and nod. "Yes, mother, my distress was brought on by you and *your* behaviour, not forgetting that of my uncle."

This time, my eyes stretch with a terrible new suspicion. No, surely not, I think.

"Mother, to be clear, Uncle Seth is my uncle, isn't he?" My palm clamps tightly over my mouth. "Please tell me now that he is."

She shakes her head, her eyes glazed while my hands begin to tremble.

"I can assure you at least that your Uncle Seth is just that. My dear girl, you have been barking up the wrong tree, driving yourself mad with a misunderstanding."

"A misunderstanding? Father didn't seem to think so. I would be grateful if you could do us the courtesy of not insulting me and his memory with yet more lies," I say.

Her head drops onto the back of the settee, and she turns her face to stare at me. She suddenly looks tired, as though life itself has been drained from her.

Perhaps the deceit has laid heavily, and she is now free of the pretence.

"Dora will be back shortly, so you must listen to me carefully, Constance." She scrabbles to sit up in her seat now as though ready to do battle. "Believe me, I had no idea you heard your father's drunken outrage. I had sent you to bed knowing where the conversation was heading if you recall."

I do recall the moment where she shooed me from the room.

"Your mind has been toying with you, I'm afraid. Let me tell you once and for all, in fact, I swear to you on my life, I *never* had an affair with your uncle."

This is only what I expected to hear if I ever dreamt about confronting her one day. I have no proof; lies are cheap, and easy to roll from the tongue.

"I'm sorry but you fail to convince me mother. Father didn't pluck his suspicions from thin air," I say.

She closes her eyes and when she opens them the mother I know has returned, her steely tenacity for justice apparent in them once more.

"If you will allow me the courtesy of listening properly to me a moment, I will explain."

She sees my silence as permission to go on with her tale, her loud sigh now ringing around the room.

"I met your Uncle Seth before I even met your father. We worked together at the foundry, and we were friendly but nothing more. Or so I thought. I discovered much later that he was hiding a secret.

I knew not so much with words but with actions that he was in love with me; the traits of love cannot be hidden forever. I chose to ignore them, however, as I couldn't reciprocate and when your father started working with us, I knew I had found the right person for me. The rest is history and I assure you my feelings towards your father never changed to the day he died, not one iota."

Her voice breaking on the last word gives me my first taste of uncertainty. I've never heard her speak in such a flowery way about love and emotion.

My lips move without words as I stare over at her, a sliver of doubt sending an icy tingle down my spine.

"But father was convinced you were having an affair. He must have known Uncle Seth was in love with you if all the signals were on show to see."

"Perhaps he did, but just because somebody thinks something it doesn't make it fact, Constance. Yes, Uncle Seth never married, and I had my concerns I had something to do with it, but I can't be held accountable for that."

A cloud darkens the room in more ways than one, rain splattering the windowpane. Dora will be back any moment, and I have so much to ask my mother still.

"But Uncle Seth was here all the time and more so when father was away, almost trying to step into his shoes I feel now. It was as though you led him on. I understand why father would think you were seeing each other behind his back when he was away at war;

you should have kept his brother at arm's length when you knew of his feelings, surely."

She clasps her hands to her cheeks. Have I discovered a loose thread in her story I wonder.

"Of that I am guilty, I admit it. I should not have allowed him to come here as much, but for both of us it was as though your father didn't feel so far away when we were together. He somehow connected us, and though we never spoke of it, I know we both found consolation from it. I waited for your uncle to call after work and cooked his tea, so it gave me a sense of normality. We were friends first and foremost after all. When your father returned from the war, like so many, he understandably wasn't himself. For my part I was just so relieved to have him home, I convinced myself time would heal him and bring the man I married back to me." A tear spills from her eye and her mouth trembles. "But in his turmoil, especially in drink he was putting two and two together and getting the wrong answer … much like you appear to have done." Her shoulders drop, and she shakes her head. "Constance, if only you had spoken to me about it."

If only I had, I think, but it was not a subject I could ever have broached, I know it still. How could I question the fidelity of my own mother?

I turn my head in the direction of the back door when it opens and Dora calls, "I'm back with the buns, grandma, there was a bit of a queue. Mrs Dobson gave me extra sweets for being so polite."

Mother's eyes are still upon me when I glance her way.

"Thank you, my dear," she calls, her voice sounding different. So much has happened in the course of the last twenty minutes.

Dora pulls her arms from her damp coat and climbs to sit on my knee, placing the buns wrapped in brown paper on the table.

I stare over her head at my mother, my resentment being rapidly quashed by a dousing of shame. I bury my face in my daughter's hair to hide from her.

There's no question in my mind any longer though this revelation will have its own repercussions …

I believe her.

Chapter 27
1931—Lawrie

My hand is touching hers on the bed cover. Barely, but it's there, and she hasn't pulled away.

I was waiting all week for an opportune moment to appear, and now it has been presented to me. I only wish the circumstances were different.

The delay risked reopening the void between us despite our brief reconciliation last Friday night.

I must uphold my end of the bargain we struck without being asked. I must speak my truth and not because I risk being discovered but because it's the right thing to do. Constance has laid herself bare and now, so should I.

I had a bittersweet unexpected reprieve. I was only too glad to delay the inevitable at first, but awaiting this moment has been like carrying a ticking bomb around my neck all week.

Fate often intervenes in life. Constance has inadvertently uncovered the truth about her mother and her uncle, the root of her being unable to recover from her father's death. This is a welcome discovery, but her guilt has now transferred to her mother and the lost years. I understand; I had avoided the rotten curse of it my entire life until a year ago.

The events of last Friday undoubtedly took us to a different place in our marriage, closer than ever, but a piece of the jigsaw is still missing. I have it in my pocket, turning it around in my hand even now for the right time to reveal it.

Last Friday we sat together in silence after all my questions had been answered. Her honesty took my breath away; it was as though she had no stopper to the outpouring of her turmoil. I love her more for it.

At some point during the early hours there was no discussion between us, but we turned off the lights both knowing it was time for bed. We undressed with our backs to each other and put on our nightclothes before sliding between the sheets. I waited, wanting to see what she would do next. Sometimes in the months before we had awoken to find ourselves entangled but generally, we stayed resolvedly on our own side of the bed.

That night was different. She turned her body towards me, leaning her forehead against my shoulder. We laid that way for some time, neither of us wanting to break the spell of our reconciliation. Her hand slid into mine eventually and I held onto it tightly as though she might slip into a ravine at any moment and into the depths of despair that she had tried to convince me she had scrambled out from. I was almost convinced. Her newfound inner confidence was only a façade, a suit of armour necessary for protection.

I was shivering, I think now from shock, even so trying to lie as still as I could when the temptation to hold her in my arms and stroke her hair threatened to overtake me. I had been starved of her for so long.

Then the hall clock struck two, those two distant chimes haunting, seemed to herald a new beginning. They almost proclaimed a fresh chapter in our marriage for me and I know Constance felt it too. She lifted her head, and I turned so our eyes joined intimately, without shame. How I'd missed the feel of her love; it was the small things like her lingering kiss before I left for work, the smile she threw me when I walked through the door on return home.

She stroked my cheek and still I didn't move, though I closed my eyes to welcome it. It was though the moment would turn to dust in my hands if I made any sudden movement. Her lips on mine were featherlight, and I wondered if they were even touching until our kiss gained impetus, convincing me it was real. Her tongue pressed between my lips, probing, searching so a groan escaped me, and I finally turned my body towards her to tangle my fingers in her hair. It was the first time I'd done so, as I would avoid touching her hair to avoid causing her any distress. She had cut it to shoulder-length only two weeks before, the waves a perfect frame for her beautiful face. When I saw it, I wanted to tell her as much, but feared she would think I preferred how she looks now more than then which is not the case.

Tearing her lips away suddenly she startled me by doing something she had never done before in all our marriage: Her legs went either side of my torso straddling me, so I was pinned to the bed. This happened to me before we met, but I assumed it would not be to her taste.

It was all so new, like the first time we made love She took me firmly between her fingers to slide me inside her, and the sensation was different, heightened soon after by the rise and fall of her body. She was in control of the movement, of everything and the shock almost overrode my excitement to begin with. This surely wasn't Constance, this wasn't my shy wife who preferred gentle lovemaking, this was a different woman, an interloper. I couldn't imagine where she had discovered such a new way of loving.

Those thoughts, however, were swept away like a ship on a breeze when it became impossible to ignore the pleasure my wife was allowing me. Our eyes locked as did our hands, and she ground her body into mine under the blueish light of the night. The strap of her nightdress slipped down her arm, so I removed one hand to reach for her breast, the soft warmth making a moan fill the silence. I closed my eyes to it until I opened them to enjoy her once more. Still our eyes held. They held until she arched her back and cried my name and I was left breathless, falling into oblivion. I can still feel her breath on my neck as she dropped forward, satiated and panting.

"I love you," she whispered, tears wetting my skin.

I raised her chin so she could see what she had done to me.

"I love you too, my darling, so much, though those words have never served me well enough."

We shared our first smile in too long. It was tired, it was poignant ... but it was ours.

Sleep eluded us as we lay on our backs, lost in thought and the afterglow of our lovemaking.

"Lawrie," she whispered, "I have something I must tell you if I'm to uphold my end of the promise.

She wanted to be completely transparent, she said for us to start afresh from that night with a clean slate.

In the darkness, she confessed then her moment of weakness as she referred to it, with Gregory Coleman.

It took more than a few seconds, but then when I unmistakably pieced together her words, I felt I had been kicked in the stomach. Her confession was utterly unexpected and shocking like being attacked in my sleep, taken unawares by an intruder. We had lost our way in our marriage, and I'm not a fool I knew someone might try to take us by the hand and lead us astray.

I reminded myself during those times, counselled myself even I was being fuelled by a jealous mind. It had never once occurred to me then that one of us might do the leading.

Where it might have led if Gregory had succumbed to my wife, I could not allow my mind the wander. Perhaps she would have seen sense before she took them to that unthinkable place.

Of course, I had disappointed Constance, she was hurt, but she was as devoted to me as I was to her, or so I thought. Our love for each other had until that moment seemed impenetrable.

Then I reminded myself that Constance no doubt thought the same once.

The girl I fell in love with, the girl I married was unrecognisable for a moment. She'd run away leaving me to tousle with my inadequacies as a husband, and premonitions of what might have been.

Perhaps then might have been the most opportune moment to tell her, but by the time I'd recovered from the shockwave, she was dozing. Her relief at finally telling me her truth will have been

221

profound, draining from her body to leave her exhausted.

Then, in the cold light of morning, my nerve had disappeared.

So, now the molehill has become a mountain in a few short days. It's time to face the girl who became a woman and tell her my story in its entirety. Somehow, I never saw her metamorphosis though I thought I was paying close attention.

Since we began our marital cleansing, I've had it pointed out that if he so chose, Gregory Coleman could hold the key to my fate … and I must not afford him the privilege.

Chapter 28
1931—Constance

"Will daddy be home for supper tonight?" Dora asks, swinging her legs from the kitchen stool and chomping away on an apple from the orchard. Her epitome of childlike innocence is tugging on my heart strings.

Mrs Osmond is ironing, the plug dangling from the ceiling lightbulb connector. The sight instils untold fear in me still and if it was up to me, I would continue warming the iron on the fire. We exchange a brief glance, before she bows her head to focus on the tablecloth she's pressing to perfection. Our relationship has changed a little of late, borne out of necessity but a welcome change, nonetheless.

"No, not tonight, sweetheart, he must still be away for work, but he's due to telephone tomorrow evening so you can speak to him then."

Her face falls the same as always when she's told the news, and I think now how I can distract her.

"Shall we go into the studio and paint? We haven't done that for ages," I ask, holding out my hand.

Her mouth forms a little 'o' and her eyes light up, so I'm delighted I came up with the idea. Dropping her apple core in the bin she grabs my hand to pull me from the kitchen.

"Well, I'll say goodnight to you both then before you take your leave, ladies," Mrs Osmond says kindly.

"Goodnight, Mrs O," we call from the hallway. "See you in the morning."

Our supper will be warming in the oven when we come down, ready for us to eat before Dora's bath and bedtime. I ensure I stick to our routine for myself as much as Dora, it's something for us to hold on to.

Mrs Osmond is familiar with us getting 'lost in the moment' as Lawrence called it, in our little art studio. It's the first time I've allowed myself to think of him in a while and so I force myself to listen to Dora informing me she's going to paint a picture of Poppy, her doll, this evening.

"What a lovely idea," I say. "I might paint her too so we can hang the paintings side by side in your bedroom. What do you think?"

She looks up at me with a furrowed brow as we step into our little hideaway.

"Don't you have to paint your other pictures for the gallery, mummy?"

She reminds me of my professional commitments, but I don't intend to think about those at present, certainly not this evening. I must ease myself into a new way of working because art cannot be forced. I've explained this to Gregory, and he's in full agreement that I must give myself time to come to terms with my new way of life.

I'd like to know if he's seen Lawrence, but I shall never ask. Gregory is keeping his powder dry, trying to maintain a neutral stance at all times.

Switching on the lamps I draw the curtains on the sleeping garden. The room is chilly but there's kindling and newspaper waiting in the fireplace for me to strike a match and light the fire. I often come here on a whim and Mrs Osmond is thoughtful enough to think ahead. The blaze is cheering the room soon enough and the tension in my neck eases a little. I check with Dora that she has everything she needs for her creation. All but water is missing for both of us, and I fetch some from the bathroom in our empty jam jars kept to hand especially for this purpose.

"Do you think Poppy should be sitting with her legs crossed for the painting," I ask in all seriousness as I move some books from the shelf to display her artfully.

"Yes, I think so," she says. "Her tatty hair could do with a tidy though, mummy, she looks like she's just got out of bed."

We giggle together, my first in weeks, months perhaps. The carefree sound is out before I can stop it then I remember why I haven't laughed in so long, and my stomach does the funny little drop like I'm falling from a great height in a dream.

I run my fingers over Poppy's unruly woollen tresses and dangle her legs from the shelf, carefully arranging one leg over the other. She wears a sailor dress of navy blue with a large white collar and red velvet bow. Her hair is dark like Dora's which is why I chose her in the first place, and she has black, beady eyes. She's a pretty, little thing much like her owner and the two have barely been separated since the day she arrived in a box for Dora's birthday three years ago. She's been a poor replacement for a sibling that never came along. I was warned after I had Dora this might be the case, but I never gave up hope. This is yet another loss I must resign myself to in my new way of life.

My throat catches as I stand at my easel, tearing off my last creation from the art pad, the one of Leeds market hall with its hustle and bustle of minute people in full flow. There is snow on the ground, the stalls filled with vibrant produce of fruit and vegetables. The city provides no end of inspiration for my work, and I pin the painting carefully to my board to sit and wait with my other works in progress. I cannot picture a day when they will be finished and displayed in what has just recently been regaled in the newspaper as the finest gallery in the north of England.

Perhaps for me that moment in the sunshine has dimmed for good.

Dora and I work in silence listening to only the crackle of the fire. In summer, the windows are open so we can enjoy the garden, so I consider it a room for all seasons.

I understand soon enough why I've been avoiding my work as my mind soon betrays me, straying to Lawrence and that awful night. My thoughts are always scurrying around, disturbing and distressing me at inopportune moments.

It was my own fault. I was the one who insisted on full disclosure, aware I would be served up an unyielding dose of reality at my own request.

*

That week was a terrible drain on my energy and spirit. I could find no peace.

Ordinarily I would have found some solace in my painting, but it wasn't enough for the first time. I decided to take a walk on the moors in the snow. I wrapped up warmly, even wearing Lawrence's oilskin coat as added protection and hours went by. I took mental images of derelict barns and winter heather-strewn landscapes to use in my work, losing track of time.

The following morning my cough started. It worsened, a fever taking hold, so I became bedridden for days. Lawrence was alarmed by how unwell I became, even insisting on taking time off from work which was unheard of and something he could ill-afford to do with all the unrest.

Sometimes, I would hear the ethereal sound of piano music as I drifted in and out of sleep. It was Lawrence playing the piano, something he hadn't done for so long and it haunted my dreams.

Mother took Dora to stay with her for a few nights which ended up being a week, Timothy was coming and going with more items for Dora as time went on.

Two days after our discussion and before I became unwell, I called to see my mother when Dora was at school. There was a change in us. Though it was early days, I would say we were speaking more as equals with me more at ease in her presence, something I'd wished for many a year. I had made a vow to make up for lost time between us, seeing it as part of our clean sheet. By then, I was ready and willing to move forward with my life and all the people in it. I only needed to speak with Lawrence.

At his insistence I stayed in bed far longer than necessary. I was becoming restless, keen to have Dora home when I was feeling so much better.

After ten days I sat up on my pillows and stared onto the snowy landscape from my bed. The pine trees beyond are our only shelter from the moorland weather and the sky had a caste, a forewarning of more snow.

Snow after Christmas always brings with it a tinge of disappointment that the festive season is behind us, but it will always be my favourite weather.

Mrs Osmond had left for the night, after Lawrence had returned home and changed, not a moment before. He was wearing his beige flannel trousers and a cream woollen pullover mother had knitted him one Christmas. It was his favourite he told her, and he wasn't only placating her. Her motherly acts have never been lost on him.

His face was ashen having slept very little. I know he worried about pneumonia setting in as mother used to when I was a child. A weak chest is always a ticking time bomb.

"You look a little better, darling," he said. "How do you feel?"

"I'll be up and about tomorrow I think," I told him, taking a sip of water.

"You mustn't rush things. Perhaps one more day in bed would be better."

"Lawrence, one more day will send me to madness," I told him with a small smile.

He sat by the bed and held my hand. I'd felt him doing that many times during my fever and it brought me comfort even when I couldn't have told him as much. We sat that way for a while looking at the snow and listening to the wind.

The bedroom was cosy and snug. I was strong enough to talk, I had been for days though Lawrence denied it, and the evening of time on our own stretched ahead.

"Lawrence, I think we must finish what we started. These last two weeks have been trying and unprecedented, but I shan't recover properly until all is said and done between us."

I saw the hollows of his eyes properly for the first time. It wasn't only tiredness I saw staring back at me; this man is in torment, I thought then. I so longed for us to be past the post then. Whatever he tells me, I'm sure I can put it behind us after all that has happened, I thought.

"We've waited long enough," I said, and he sighed and nodded in defeat as he looked back out of the window, his jaw clenched.

I studied his beautiful profile. Dark shadows or not, he was still the most handsome man I had ever laid eyes upon. My mind flew then to Daphne Farrington as it always did, I had come to realise.

"Do you consider me to be a good man?" he asked quietly.

It was an oddly unexpected question to be asked, but one easy enough to answer.

"Of course I do," I said in all honesty.

He turned to look at me, his eyes scouring my face for clues.

"Do you think I've been a good husband?"

"What is this, Lawrie, the Spanish inquisition?" I asked a note of trepidation by then in my tone.

"Do you though?"

I thought about how to answer, my expression speaking volumes no doubt without any need for words.

"I know what you're thinking," he said, "and it's not a trick question. You think I was a good husband, but now I've put a foot wrong. Perhaps you also wonder if all our marriage has been a sham."

I was taken aback by his succinct appraisal of exactly how I had been feeling about us for months. But then I remembered how once we had always been able to second-guess each other's moods and emotions.

"It was a little more than putting a foot out of line. If you recall, there was a question mark over you fathering a child to someone else," I said.

Sitting up straight suddenly, he looked me straight and true in the eye.

"I think I just need to explain, Constance. We have pussy-footed around each other long enough and it isn't doing either of us any good."

A sense of urgency coiled itself around me. That was what I wanted, and the moment had arrived.

"So, explain it to me. I need to know for my own sanity what is going on between you and Daphne Farrington. Explain to me why you have allowed the woman to become a cloud over our marriage."

Surely the truth cannot be worse than my own imagination, I thought.

He got up to walk over to the bedroom; the room had become his confessional box, and like a sinner he needed a barrier from the priest.

"Daphne Farrington took me by surprise the Christmas Eve before last when she told me about being in love with me. This you now know. For my part, I was reeling, having no clue of how she felt. I rebuked her as gently as I could but, however tactful my approach, it was still a rejection.

I think now I should have accepted her decision to resign when she landed on the doorstep that Boxing Day, but I was confident that we were grown-ups who could handle the situation respectfully. More importantly, I knew and still know how much she loved her job, it was her whole life and obviously she wasn't having a baby at that point. I would have felt like I'd pushed her out of her role, which only seemed unfair."

I knew that much about her, at least. However, I always sensed from the outset her feelings for my husband were more than of a professional and platonic nature. Lawrence was clearly oblivious. The two of them spent many hours together, and I mistakenly assumed that our getting married would put an end to any hope she may have harboured.

Lawrence dropped his head then, saying, "I was disgusted by what she did to you, and she knew it, but it was too late by the time I found out the truth. She left the night Gregory disclosed the rumours and even before, I knew immediately who was behind them. She had let both of us down and she was well aware of it. That time is so difficult to recall. The only good thing that came out of it was that it prompted a change for you and your ... frame of mind."

That point I cannot deny, I thought then, taking another sip of water. I knew all that he had confessed so far though the knot in my stomach was still tightening.

"If you remember, we had run out of ideas for a resolution, and you were if not depressed then suffering from intense anxiety. Now I know the extent, it terrifies me what may have come to pass if we had been unable to find a way forward. I hope it goes without saying that I wish it could have happened differently, but the fact remains it spurred you into a course of action and I was relieved, and incredibly proud of how you seemed to triumph over adversity."

I remembered how desperate we were; I was spending too long crying in the dark when I was alone, caught in a cycle with no beginning and no end. There was Dora to think of and I'm amazed now how I managed to hide it all from her.

"The main thing I've learned in all this, the crux of the sorry tale if you will, is that you often don't realise how important a person is to you until they're removed from your life. I had seen her day in, day out for far longer than you even. I leaned on her professionally and she had become more than an assistant…but this is what I must make abundantly clear: I was never in love with her. You must believe me on this point, or we're doomed to never move forward."

A cold hand squeezed my heart so tightly I stopped breathing a moment. To think my husband was pining for another woman in any capacity was a crushing blow when I was laid low. Perhaps I should have waited, but I still wanted us to plough on.

He turned to face me, hands in pockets as I tried to swallow down my pain. I was determined not to cry, or it would have thrown him off-course. We both knew it was vital we reached the end of his story that night.

"You've told me of the situation with Gregory Coleman and …" he said, before I broke him off.

"Lawrence, please do not divert the attention from yourself. I'm paying my penance for the failures in our marriage and now it's time for you to do the same."

"I shall, but please answer me this if you will: If Gregory was in trouble, would you feel obligated to help him in spite of him being a man, and in spite of me?"

I considered his words carefully. Gregory was another human being, a friend, and I knew then I would never be able to turn my back on him should he find himself in any difficulty or distress.

"The difference is, I think I would have spoken to you about it first, rather than going behind your back," I said.

Sighing, he turned his face towards the window once again, the barrier back in position.

"Perhaps you would, and I know I should have done the same, but you were in a terrible place, Constance. I was petrified of pushing you over the edge."

"Then would it not have been better to dismiss her the moment you discovered she was pregnant, despite your platonic feelings for her," I said. "Then at least, there would never have been a grey area relating to the paternity of her child."

"Constance, don't you see, it would have been like abandoning a younger sister who had fallen from grace, throwing her to the wolves of society and walking away without a glance over my shoulder?"

He flew to my side, his Adam's apple bobbing manically up and down. I couldn't be sure if he was angry or upset.

"Are you saying that you have been unable to abandon her, Lawrie, that … that you're still seeing her now?" I whispered.

"No, I swear I haven't seen her for quite some time," he said.

That was not what I asked, and he knew it by his eyes dropping to the floor.

"So, you're saying you have seen her since she left?" I asked, almost unable to say the words aloud.

There were tears in his eyes when he looked at me then, the pain behind them immeasurable.

"Please, Constance, I hope you will allow me the chance to explain," he said.

His expression told me it went far beyond some harmless, if inappropriate meetings … and I could never be ready for what I silently prayed would surely be his final revelation.

Chapter 29
1931—Lawrie

"How many times did you see her after she left work?" Constance asked.

The words fired from her tongue as though she'd been holding them in too long and needed to be rid of them.

I sat in the chair by her bed and thought carefully of my next words.

She had been so unwell, fitful in her sleep and I'd never encountered how bad the bouts of bronchitis could be. I dozed in the chair most nights, waking with a sickly panic to check she was still with me. Her mother told me that was what it could be like when she was a child, but the purer air out here, away from the city had helped.

"Lawrence," she said then.

"I never saw her on a regular basis, I only checked to see how she was on a number of occasions." I deliberated briefly whether to lie for her sake, but those weren't the rules of this game. "Perhaps four," I said.

Her eyebrows shot upwards but then down again so quickly I would have missed it if I wasn't staring at her. Her reaction told me it was less than she had imagined.

"Did you… did you ever sleep with her on your visits?"

My face flew in her direction.

"No, never!" I said, alarm coating my words. I'd been waiting for the question, and I had to convince her. "On my own life, on Dora's life, you are the only woman I have ever made love to, Constance. You must believe me."

I stared into her eyes a long second to convince her. I didn't say "made love to in the true sense" because she knew exactly what I meant. I have only ever been in love with Constance.

She was convinced, I could tell by the relief showing on her face.

"There's more though, isn't there?" she said flatly, as though she had no more energy left in her body to draw on. I watched her a moment to see if I really should go on, to see if she was as strong as she professed to be after her illness. She sat waiting for me to continue.

Memories flooded my mind as I turned to face the fire.

"When I first met you, I found your shy, faltering ways endearing. I'd never been affected by someone so instantly and so profoundly; it was as if a light within you was shining only for me. As we've discussed many times, it was wonderful yet disconcerting."

The leaping flames of the fire drew me in, so I was back in those heady early days of our courtship. Her silence made me sense she had granted me permission to meander back to those special times with me.

"Even then I sensed you had hidden depths. It turned out to be far more than I could ever have predicted, and it drew me to you. I yearned to see your smile; it was so elusive at first and now I know why.

"Remember the day I proposed. That was when your true uncompromised smile appeared for the first time as you looked at the ring on your finger. I felt in that moment I would want to chase it forever."

I closed my eyes briefly to the fact that life was so solid and straightforward then, traits I knew were lost to us.

"It was understandable that you were worried about your hair, any person would be. In time I thought I had convinced you it made no difference to me, simply because it *didn't* make any difference. You grew to almost feel part of me and if you could have accepted yourself that way, I would have gladly lived with that beautiful woman, that beautiful person forever."

I glanced over and caught her eye in the lamplight.

"Lawrie, I was broken in pieces then, my hair loss only part of my anxiety."

She sat up, so the coverlet slipped down to her waist, showing her lace bed jacket.

"Are you telling me you loved me more then, when I was broken; that you preferred that person?"

I shook my head, a panic taking hold about how I could explain myself adequately.

"It wasn't like that, Constance. I wanted you well, of course I did. I mistakenly hoped time and my love would mend you. My wish for you came true, you have become stronger, more independent, and that's how it should be."

237

I wasn't making my point well because I was still trying to come to terms with how we had become different people myself.

"Then I don't understand. I only changed because it was forced on me by others, yourself included."

"So, it seems we are damned either way," I said, "I want us to feel the same when everything is changed, but believe me, I never wanted you to remain in the place you were then."

She sighed and put a hand to her forehead, saying, "That young girl is gone to you, Lawrie, like the man you were is gone to me. We must accept it or … or suffer the alternative.

She stopped short of spelling it out but there can be no misunderstanding. I can't lose her, I thought then, distress taking a chokehold of me, chilling me to the core.

"When I visited Daphne Farrington last July, it was the hottest day of the year. She was bloated and struggling with the extreme heat as you might imagine. I called with some sandwiches and lemonade, that's all. She was so close to the end of her pregnancy and living alone. I know you might say that was her choice, but it was still her reality."

Constance's eyes glistened my way. I ran my hands down my face and sat back in the armchair, crossing my bent calf over my opposite thigh. I would do anything not to have to relive the moment, I thought, playing with a stray thread at the ankle of my trousers.

"We ate our sandwiches and chatted about the latest perfume range for autumn in the store. She had a few ideas about Christmas displays she'd thought of the year before, and I was keen to listen as always. That was how we communicated, about work matters and nothing more.

Anyway, I digress. She left to go to the bathroom, and I checked my watch. It was time for me to leave to get back to work, so I got up to put the plates in the sink. I thought about how different life had been for us when we were having Dora. I just couldn't help feeling pity for her as I waited for her to return. I think now pity was the overriding emotion I have felt for her the past year."

I was stalling again, heaving a breath before continuing.

"From the sitting room I heard a yell coming from the direction of the bathroom and I ran toward it.

She shouted that the baby was coming. I was like a rabbit caught in the headlights for a second or two until all mayhem ensued."

Constance's eyes widened, so a tear escaped down her cheek, but she didn't utter a word while the ending of my tale was unfolding.

"Panicking, I tried the door, but it was locked. I should have run to the telephone in the hallway and called for a midwife but all I could think about in that moment was opening the door. I pushed with my shoulder it seemed no end of times and then I raised my foot and kicked it, finally gaining entry.

She was crouched on the bathroom tiles, her face puce and pouring with sweat. I told her I'd call for help, but she begged me not to leave. I was out of my depth as much as she was. I…"

"Stop!" Constance said then, holding up her hand. "I can well imagine the rest of what happened, and I'd much prefer it if you spared me the graphic details."

She sat forward in bed, holding a hand to her chest, her wet face on fire.

"Are you now telling me that you delivered that woman's baby?"

Her tone made me shudder, though it was only what I had expected.

"Not entirely, no, I made a telephone call from the hallway after persuading her I would return immediately. The operator put me through to the doctor, and two midwives arrived in the nick of time. I was never more thankful to see anyone."

Constance's gaze was steady, yet still somehow shriveling me inside.

"But you were in the vicinity for most of the birth?"

I stared at her a moment then nodded only to confirm the obvious outcome.

She swung her legs out of bed to get up and I thought for a moment she might collapse until she sat down again.

"So, you went on numerous occasions to see another woman behind my back which is bad enough, but it just so happens that this particular woman has caused me no end of trauma, and now … now you're telling me that you were present when she had her baby. A baby I might add I have been told by both suspected parties involved is not yours, yet you seem to care so much about the child you would humiliate me in this way."

I had imagined Constance saying these words, or a variation of them many times. When I laid awake fretting, I knew I would have to tell her one day. It was the right thing to do, even without the risk of Gregory telling her or simply letting the cat out of the bag myself.

I regret confiding in him before all the upset, but in those days, he was my valued confident. He had never disclosed my secret, but what of the future? What if we quarrelled, and he wanted to exact some kind of revenge? I could not live with such a risk following me around day after day when finding out third hand would surely be worse for her.

I reminded myself that Gregory has done nothing wrong to me or to Constance. The damage we have done has been of our own doing.

Constance shook her head, her lips a hard line of disgust. The look in her narrowed eyes is something I shall never forget.

Yet, I deserved every ounce of it.

"I know I'm not entirely blameless in this debacle, and I suppose I should only be grateful you haven't been unfaithful in the usual, tawdry sense. But in a different way this feels the same. Unwittingly or otherwise, you now share a bond so … so intimate. I can't bear it, Lawrence, you weren't even present at Dora's birth. It's too much."

Tears were rolling freely down her face, and I was helpless, the last person who could provide her with any comfort. I knew it would be better for me to keep my distance and not aggravate her pain.

"It's little consolation, but I never planned what happened and if I could change it tomorrow, I would."

It sounded the same as if I was apologising for an affair, even to me.

I would change it, but I was unable to deny the pull the child had on me. I've refrained from seeing him since that day in the park, because it would be unfair on all of us, most of all him. I recall his scrunched, tiny face as he bawled when the midwife put him in my arms so she could settle Daphne. She brought him into the living room, the oppressive heat meaning he only wore a napkin, so his fresh baby skin was next to my hands and forearm. He was a new life and though I wish it were different I was affected by it.

"I don't think there's much more to be said," Constance said then, wiping her eyes with the back of her hand.

She sat staring at the bedside rug for so long and all the while I didn't move a muscle.

"Lawrence," she said finally, "I think we need some time apart. I can see no other way under the circumstances."

Of all the things I expected her to say or do, things I had imagined over the months, this was never on the list.

"Please, Constance, if I go, I don't think you will ever let me return. Do you want that for us?"

She laid back on the pillows and stared at the ceiling.

"I've no idea what I want, but at this moment I can't bring myself to look at you. It's the final straw, Lawrence and I think it for the best." She paused and turned her head away to look out into the darkness. "I would be grateful if you could be gone by morning.

242

I'll tell Dora you've been called away on business, she'll be none the wiser at the age she is, thank goodness for small mercies. If you let Timothy know where you intend staying, he can collect more of your things."

I was shivering uncontrollably by then, her dismissive tone adding another layer to my shame. What a terrible mess I had made, and yet I could only look on and observe with no power in me to clean it up.

"You think you don't know me any longer, Lawrence, but believe me, the feeling is entirely mutual," she said quietly.

My head dropped into my hands, my breathing too loud in my ears.

Her instructions were so well executed, so precise I knew in that moment my wife had been thinking about the possibility of us separating for some time, perhaps in the trying weeks running up to Christmas. Was it then that she met with Daphne I wondered.

Regardless … now all is said and done, what does it matter any longer?

Chapter 30
1931—Constance

Mother stepped down from the tram, oblivious to me waiting outside *Jenny Wren's* for her to arrive.

She smiled when she saw me, raising her hand and I did the same. This is the first time we've done something together, something that any mother and daughter might do often and even take for granted.

I need a new dress for a little soiree Gregory has planned at the gallery and thought we might choose it together.

"It's time you ventured out, and this will be the perfect opportunity, Constance. You can't hide away for the rest of your life," he said when he telephoned at the weekend with the invitation.

I can't help thinking we have unfinished business, but then it was more important that I finished my business with Lawrence first. He needs to see Dora, so I know we must talk in the near future. At least that's how I feel today, but tomorrow might be different.

"Well, this makes a pleasant change," I say to mother as she arrives at the shop, handbag tucked away tidily under her arm. It perfectly matches her taupe coat and hat, which isn't unusual, but her new shade of lipstick shows me she's made a special effort.

"Indeed, it does You look nice, Constance, is that a new coat?" she asks.

It isn't, but she hasn't seen me wearing it before, I tell her. We're being rather polite, but this is all new and strange for both of us.

Jennifer is wrapping a new acquisition for a customer at the counter when we enter the shop. She greets us with a smile, and mother and I browse the racks while we wait for her to finish.

"Hello, Mrs Crawford," Jennifer says when the customer leaves us. "I haven't seen you in here for a while."

What she really means is I haven't seen you in here ever because mother buys her clothes from *British Home Stores* in town and nowhere else. I'm hoping she'll allow me to treat her today, though she doesn't know it.

"You're doing rather well for yourself, Jennifer," mother says with a genuine smile. "Your mother must be very proud. How is she by the way?"

"Oh, you know mam, she's always the same. You're right though, she's pleased as punch with how well the shop is doing. We all are."

I subdue a little smile, finding it comical how differently Jennifer speaks to her customers. She never puts on airs and graces with us.

"I've put one or two things aside for you, Connie. Wait there, I'll get them from the back."

As I watch her walk away, I think how relieved I am that nothing has come of the warning she received from *Lewis's* solicitors. Daphne Farrington trespasses my thoughts, and I'm disappointed to find her wandering around my mind yet again. I wonder how to distract myself before she takes a firm grasp of it.

"Is this to your taste?" I ask mother now, holding up a dress I spotted last week for her to see. She nods her approval.

"Yes, it's lovely, but I'm not sure it's quite me. Anyway, Constance I'm not in need of any new clothes, I have plenty."

"I'd like to treat you though … if you'll let me," I say, holding the dress against her. "I suspect you'll say no, but it would make my day if you accepted a little gift just this once."

Her eyebrows raise before her head drops to look at the new dress. It has a light brown skirt and a cream blouse top with a bow at the neck, quite conservative but a little more special than the dresses she normally wears.

"I've no idea on what occasion I would wear something like this. It will only sit in my wardrobe gathering dust," she says, eyes still studying the dress closely.

"Well, I was thinking of going for afternoon tea with Dora to the *Wellesley* if you'd care to join us, Jennifer too," I say as she arrives with two dresses hanging over her arm.

"Constance, you have enough to worry about surely without organising afternoon tea," mother says, although not unkindly.

She's quite right, but I must keep my mind occupied and tell mother as much. To be perfectly honest, if it was left up to me, I would struggle to get out of my bed at the moment. I cannot afford a relapse when I've only just freed myself from the teeth of the black dog for Dora's sake.

"Have you heard anything from Lawrie?" Jennifer asks now.

Oh dear, I had hoped to enjoy a reprieve from the separation. It appears my wish is not to be fulfilled.

"We haven't spoken directly but before you say it, I know we must, and we shall."

Jennifer, who knows the full story, purses her lips into a sad smile. Mother only knows part of it and I'm still unsure whether to enlighten her.

It surprised me she hasn't completely taken Lawrie's side as I was expecting. That's not to say she condones separation, believing a husband and wife should be able to work out their problems under the same roof.

"Come on," I say in the lightest tone I can muster, "let's try these dresses on and then have a nice cup of tea."

In the cubicle I slip on the first dress, thinking I have mixed feelings about the soiree Gregory has organised. I know he's trying to pull me back into the outside world, but I'm not certain I'm quite ready to make chit chat and hobnob with strangers.

Despite my best efforts, I miss Lawrie more than I care to admit. He has wronged me, but it hasn't stopped me longing for his reassuring touch, his powerful presence, just the nearness of him. Night times are bad enough when my mind is unable to stop replaying our conversations in the loneliness of the dark, but when I wake to an empty bed, the feeling is worse.

Dora is accepting of the situation, but she has started to ask a few questions about her father's return. Though she's young, I'm trying my best not to be overly secretive. Secrets created this sorry situation in the first place.

Lawrence will be missing her more.

I have a sudden recollection of Dora padding into our bedroom one night when life was different, telling us she was fearful of the wind.

"It sounds like it's in my room, mummy," she said. "It's too loud."

Poppy was hanging from her hand, Dora's plaited hair falling over her shoulders like a dainty doll herself.

"Come lay with me a while," I said, and she hopped on the bed, moulding her tiny, warm body into mine.

Lawrie lay close to me, reaching over to stroke Dora's hair.

"You know, sometimes the wind gets lonely, out there on his own all the time," he said. "He likes to visit from the moors and whistle hello down the chimney, that's all."

Dora turned her face to look at her daddy unsmiling.

"Can he come inside the house?" she asked, her little cheeks pinched with concern.

"No, never but he likes us to know he's there. I love the wind; he makes me sleepy."

Dora's round eyes glazed as she pondered about the wind being a new friend.

"Shall we go listen to him together?" Lawrie asked. "I might even be able to tell you what he's saying if we listen very carefully."

She smiled and nodded, her smile returning, so I kissed her goodnight and watched them leave the room hand in hand. Lawrie has always been an involved father; it must be terrible for him being apart from her. He was so young when his mother died; the notion of him growing up without her haunts me still despite everything.

I listened that night to the hum of their voices in the room next door as I waited for Lawrie to return. The sense of safety and security I took for granted is now gone.

A panic suddenly rises in me. Pressing a hand to my breast I try to subdue my breathing and stem the flow of tears. I must waltz from the cubicle in a moment and play the part of a woman who is in control of her life, so her mother and best friend will not worry themselves to distraction.

The still air in the small cubicle is swaddling me tightly, so each breath is short and laboured.

It's clear I have been in denial. I've now discovered that secrets have the power to crush something that was once pure and wonderful into dust.

Then one day it just blows away and scatters to the wind.

Chapter 31
1931—Lawrence

I try not to detest my new home because I know it could be worse. *The Beech Hotel* is an old manor house, not too far from the leafy suburb of Alwoodley.

It's nestled in a tree-lined avenue and flanked by other grand houses of the wealthy. In the past I'd recommended the hotel to associates who travelled to Leeds for meetings having heard about it from Stephen Tobin. I was grateful to discover it lived up to its excellent reputation for service and importantly, discretion. It was the only place I could think to go at such short notice.

I am situated close enough yet far enough from work and there's nobody other than Gregory connected with *Lewis's* who knows my personal affairs. I've been staying there almost three weeks trying to make the best of it.

Timothy dutifully calls to collect me each morning and I look forward to seeing his familiar face and having the banal chat about the weather or the news. It has become the highlight of my day and when he drops me back at the hotel of an evening—as late as possible without prolonging his day unnecessarily—a sense of emptiness grips me as the car drives away.

When Timothy came with more of my personal belongings the first time, there was a surprise, or perhaps a shock waiting for me. The box was strategically placed in my suitcase so I could not miss it. I opened it knowing what was inside already ... my monogrammed cufflinks. I'd taken them home in case Daphne spotted them in my draw and was upset by my ingratitude. I thought then it was the end of the matter; how foolish I was.

In not wishing to cause offence, I had only done far greater damage.

I eat alone in the hotel restaurant pretending to read a book, and the staff are unintrusive. The weekends loom, and Sunday is a gaping chasm of nothing and nobody. I often wander into work entering via the rear entrance to go up to my office. It's a welcome chance to be alone so I can drink a glass or two of whisky without being cooped up in my hotel room or surrounded by strangers in a public house. I scold myself that this is a bad habit to form, yet still I do it.

I call the house most evenings to speak to Dora after Mrs Osmond answers the telephone. She places the receiver down and I hear her tip tapping on the tiles as she goes in search of my daughter, picturing the scene in my mind's eye.

Dora arrives after a few moments to tell me of her day, finishing with the same little ditty she sings to me in her childlike voice:

"Mamas in the kitchen,
Doing a bit of stitching,
In ran a bogeyman,
And she ran out!"

Every night I exclaim how lovely she sings the song. I mean it. Soon I must see her; I have been patient, but it's been too long. This I know will mean reopening the lines of communication with her mother.

A nasty little voice has been whispering in my ear that Constance may be seeking solace from Gregory in my absence. In drink, this voice grows loud enough to deafen me, so I think I might go mad with it. Those nights I walk to the telephone in my office and pick up the receiver. I stare at in my shaking hand before returning it to the cradle with a slam. This is then my cue to return to the hotel on the tram to sleep it off.

Gregory unexpectedly called into my office last week. His approach of pretending everything was normal suited me fine, and I went along. He had good news he told me, something that was sure to cheer me.

"I see, and what might that be?" I asked dully, pouring two whiskies from the decanter.

He reached to take his tumbler from me with a wry smile.

"You had better sit down," he said, his legs crossed in a relaxed manner, and a playful look in his eye.

I joined him by the fire, and we raised our glasses before taking more than a sip of the fiery blend.

"Well, wait for it … Daphne Farrington, no less came in to see old Tobin last week."

I clattered my glass down on the side table and sat forward, keen to know more, and quickly.

"Daphne; I never saw her. Why on earth should this be good news for me, Gregory?"

He shrugged his shoulders, handing me a broad grin, so he looked almost boyish. My mind went to Constance and her almost succumbing to those charms I see now.

"She made an appointment to meet before opening time to discuss a very important matter. I saw her on her way out briefly. I now have it straight from the horse's mouth that she came to discuss the matter of your good reputation."

I felt the drop of my jaw, and my cheeks blazed no doubt aided by the warmth of the fire and the whisky. Daphne met with the Managing Director of *Lewis's* to discuss my reputation; I couldn't possibly make sense of it.

"What on earth did she say, do you know?" I asked Gregory eventually.

He raised an eyebrow, the intrigue making my tongue glue to the roof of my mouth despite the whisky.

"I'm paraphrasing of course, but principally, she told Stephen you are most certainly *not* the father of her child and you have been nothing but kind to her. She admitted making mischief before leaving her post and now regrets the repercussions of it. You're in the clear, Lawrence, once and for all. I never doubted it for a minute, but then not everybody knows you as I do."

The remark cut me when I realised my wife is now included in the 'everybody' he mentioned. Gregory was oblivious, only too delighted to be the bearer of good news.

"Did you hear me, old boy? You're in the clear at last, that must be one thing off your plate at least."

It absolutely was, and I should have been elated, but my reputation was and is the least of my worries at present. My wife's opinion of me is my only concern.

My thoughts must have been plain as a pikestaff.

"She cares for you, Lawrence, just as you care for her," he said. "You'll work it out between you, I know it. I'm not just spouting platitudes to appease you; I hope a reconciliation will happen before too long."

I got up from my seat to refill our glasses though his was still half full. He looked slightly perturbed, but I had to get away from him or risk breaking down and humiliating myself. Of course, I was happy to hear the news, but could not see that anything in my personal life would be changed by it.

"Have you seen Constance?" I asked at the drink's cabinet, my back toward him.

There was a rub of leather as he adjusted position in his seat, perhaps a sign of discomfort, I wondered.

"No, I haven't seen her. She hasn't been to the gallery as she's not feeling very focused on her artwork at present. I imagine she has the equivalent of writer's block. We've spoken on the telephone once, but it was purely business other than the barest mention of you not being at home."

"I see," I said, deliberating how the subject of me was broached. I was unsure then whether to pose the question lurking within … but in the end, I did.

"May I ask you something, Gregory?"

He deliberated for too long as I waited with the crystal top of the decanter in my hand.

"If you feel you must," he said finally.

I must, I thought instantly though I was still unsure what could be propelling me.

"If Constance and I should … should separate for good, might I ask if you will look after her? I don't like to think of her on her own, that's all."

I closed my eyes as I waited for his answer and a tear slid down my cheek onto my lapel.

"Lawrie, please, don't do this to yourself, there's no need. You will both be back on track soon and then mark my words you will regret having this conversation with me."

His short laugh did nothing to convince me there was humour behind his words.

"Will you? I asked again, undeterred, keeping my voice in check. I somehow had to know the answer, it was imperative.

There was no response while my heart pounded and I waited … and waited. Eventually I heard his muffled footsteps on the carpet and the click of the door closing.

Only then did my chin drop to my chest as I wept for the third time in as many weeks.

But that time I was alone, and I had never felt it more in my life.

Chapter 32
1931—Constance

The gallery is lit but deserted when I arrive. I must be the first I think, recalling the agenda with Gregory. He said seven o'clock I'm certain of it.

Checking my lipstick in my compact mirror, I fluff my hair and look down at my new dress of salmon pink shimmering under the lights. A perfect choice of Jennifer's, and I didn't have the will to try on the second dress she chose due to being overcome with my disturbing thoughts of a time gone by. I shake the memory from my shoulders.

"Hello," I call now as I wander amongst the wonderful display of paintings Gregory has collected from far and wide. I spot only one of my creations, a blank space below where the ticket should be, denoting a recent sale he must have been remiss in telling me about.

"Hello, Constance."

I recognise the voice immediately and stay perfectly still a moment. When I gather the strength to turn around slowly, Lawrie is standing before me in a dinner jacket. It looks like new and he's clean shaven, his hair freshly cut. My heart and my stomach fight for my attention. The only clue to him being the Lawrie I saw last are the dark shadows under his eyes still.

"Lawrence," I say, trying to keep a monotone. "What brings you here this evening?"

His unexpected appearance affects me, and I wonder now where on earth Gregory might have got to.

"If you would be good enough to step into Gregory's office, I will be glad to explain," he says, stepping to one side.

My legs are unable move. I will feel as though he has backed me into a corner if I go inside that room. We stare at each other, my mind racing through the possible scenarios. Is Gregory ill; has the event been cancelled for some reason?

"I hope you will forgive us, but Gregory and I brought you here under false pretences. It was his idea, offering us a private place to talk away from … home."

His hesitation surrounding the last word is not lost on me. So, Gregory has been in cahoots with my husband, I can scarcely believe it. But then I forget Gregory has a vested interest in my career, and I have been somewhat elusive of late.

I close my eyes and sigh quietly, admitting defeat. If Lawrence and I don't speak now, it must be later, and the moment will only loom until it happens like it has been for weeks.

"Well, I suppose tonight is as good a time as any," I say, heading in the direction of Gregory's office. I recall the last time I was here; so much has happened since. In a few short weeks that woman has lived a lifetime.

A bottle of champagne sits in an ice bucket, alongside two glasses and a selection of elegant canapes on a silver stand. There's a welcoming fire burning in the grate and a bowl of red roses on the desk.

"All his own work," Lawrie says almost coyly.

Despite my anxiety and better judgement, a small smile lifts my lips.

"Or perhaps Mrs Fisher's," I say, and he returns my smile before we look quickly away, forgetting ourselves for a moment.

"Champagne?" Lawrie asks and I nod, watching him then expertly open the bottle and pour the drink into the crystal glasses. He hands me a one and raises his saying, "To … moving forward."

I raise my glass but avoid looking into his eyes, even though I know some consider this to be bad luck. This way my eyes won't betray my scepticism. We sit down opposite one another, and I arrange my dress before I settle.

Ordinarily, this is the moment he would say something about how beautiful my dress is or something similar, but he only stares at the bubbles in his champagne.

"Well, I thought I knew how to start the conversation, having the upper hand in knowing we would meet tonight, but I'm afraid you have me at a loss," he says.

This is not the confident Lawrie of old, the one who knows how to roll with the moment effortlessly. My throat tightens when I think how changed he is.

The thought is soon swallowed by the contradiction that this situation is of his own making, and on and on it might go, spinning on a loop, like most nights when I lay awake.

"How is Dora?" he asks.

"She's fine, but she misses you," I say, the candid statement taking me by surprise. "I think it only right that you see her this weekend. I can only apologise for not being able to bring myself to face you, it was unfair on both of you."

He casts his eyes my way but only briefly.

"It's been a trying time for us; I understand why we needed time apart."

I feel my brows knit as I watch him.

"Time apart? This has not been a trial separation, Lawrence. I miss you terribly, but I'm not sure we shall be able to simply pick up where we left off after a few weeks."

His crestfallen expression tweaks my conscience.

"Forgive me for my inappropriate choice of words. I too have wondered of late if we will ever find it in us to be happy together again."

My heart leaps to the back of my throat. Not for one moment did I think he was having doubts, I thought us reconciling or otherwise would be entirely my own decision.

"I see, and here was I convinced your love for me was unwavering, never in question."

There's a hint of vulnerability in my words; I'm irritated with myself for allowing it.

"My love is just that, as I know yours is also unwavering. However, the premise of love can change between a couple over the course of a lifetime. I realise this now having had no end of time to dwell on what has unfolded between us."

Tears sting my eyes and I take a large sip of champagne before placing my glass down.

"How has your loved changed, Lawrence?" I ask, a tremble running through my words.

"Constance, if I were to go home with you tonight, I wonder what we would have resolved? We have changed but quickly, not over many years. I take the blame unreservedly for my underhand approach in trying to protect … people in such a clumsy manner. But the marriage we had has gone."

Gone. Of course it has, but this brutal statement of the obvious churns my stomach. My strength and composure are dispersing, running away when I need them the most.

"I see you have given the state of our marriage considerable thought and drawn an unsettling conclusion without any help from me. I feel now as though I've been ambushed," I say, my bottom lip quivering so I clamp it tightly between my teeth.

"I assure you I have done no such thing. I have brought you here to apologise and to move us along to our next chapter… for Dora's sake, but also for our own sake. We must be truthful. A new kind of marriage is the only option for us now, but I would very much like us to have it because my love for you remains as solid as ever. The question is, are you of the same mind knowing we can never return to those days?"

A pain is crushing my chest like the day I finally resigned myself to never seeing my father again. It bore down heavily, so I staggered backwards onto the bed, the tightness so intense I was unable even to weep.

This is how I feel right now. The Lawrence and Constance of old are gone forever and will never return no matter how much I wish it, just like my father.

I sense his eyes on me, watching, waiting.

Perhaps I expected him to be a crumbling shell of a man when we met. I spot the signs of sleepless nights and lack of food but what I have always admired most about Lawrie are his strength of mind and pragmatism, but also his empathy. He sobbed at my feet only weeks ago when he discovered the depths of the despair I'd lived with for twelve years.

Today, he is searching for a way forward for us and this is all we can hope for.

"As you know, I went to see her," I say after a moment. "It was one thing causing me distress, but quite another when she involved Jennifer. A line had been crossed, Lawrie, I had no option but to act. I called at her flat and confronted her, expecting a quarrel, but it never materialised. She was rather humble and apologetic."

"That will have taken some courage on your part. I'm obviously upset she was mean-spirited enough to do such a thing. You must have struck a chord however, because since your meeting, she has met with Stephen Tobin to set the record straight." A snort escapes him. "My reputation has been restored … for the little it matters now."

I think about the hastily scribbled note I wrote asking her to do as much. I had no desire to see her with her child and now I'm especially glad I didn't see him after discovering my husband's involvement in his entrance into the world.

"So, it appears she honoured my request," I say, experiencing a slight shift, a fresh understanding of the situation.

He shakes his head, a strange expression on his face, saying, "Yet again you surprise me, Constance. I could never have imagined you confronting anyone only months ago." He pauses. "This is yet another example of how changed we are."

"Well, I assure you I have told you everything now, my slate is wiped clean," I say. "Tell me now if you have anything else to add."

How I hope not, I will have to leave if he has.

"None whatsoever, you know all there is to know. I wish I could say I feel better for unburdening myself, but it would be a lie."

My smile is weak, his weaker still as our eyes melt.

"You look very beautiful tonight," he says.

My cheeks burn from the bubbles, or perhaps under his admiring gaze which is raw and unsettling.

"Your confidence has grown so you seem quite at ease in the spotlight. The Constance I once knew hated the limelight, she only wanted to sit by the fire and talk as we are now. She wanted to paint in her studio and was never happier than when she was at home."

My eyes burn with tears when I remember that girl.

"I miss her too," I whisper. "The limelight went to my head a little I think."

He drops to my knees and takes my hands, so I'm startled by it.

"She's still there, only she wants a little more from life. I'd like her to have it too."

His eyes darting between my own are sparkling with tears as I grip his hands as though he might run away.

"And what if you don't like this new version?" I ask, the question so pressing I know he will feel he has nowhere to turn.

"I love her already," he says without hesitation.

"Yes, but can you love her in the long term? You had never seen the confident Constance, but I had never seen the jealous, possessive Lawrence. It was worse because you had no right to be when so much was going on I didn't know about …"

"… which is exactly my point. We need to create a solid foundation first before we can even think about building on it. All I know is, we have learnt so much. I accept my part and all I can do is apologise for the last time and promise you it was a lapse in judgement that will never happen again. The only woman I have ever loved as a man should love a woman is you, Constance, nobody else. Even now I know there could never be anyone for me but you, and my jealousy was fear of losing you, nothing more. I'm ashamed of my churlish behaviour, but I thought you didn't need me any longer."

Me losing him; him not needing me any longer, I have lived with the very same fears since the day we met, so I empathise, I think as he stares unblinkingly into my eyes. He is so handsome, yet so good-hearted … an attractive combination which I worried about being snatched from me every day.

Tonight, has brought it home to me that I worry still. I convinced myself I had the moral high ground, and that was enough to have him beg me to take him back.

"Will we be compromised, settling for something less?" I ask, a tear hurtling down my face unchecked.

He takes his handkerchief from his pocket and dabs my cheek gently.

"I don't see it as something less, only something else," he sighs, a small smile on his lips now, "Constance, I admit I've been a mess without you, and I never want to have a taste of it again."

He hands me his handkerchief before rising to his full height.

"But only you can know the answer to that question. I hoped we might trust each other at least enough to build on it. In truth, neither of us has done anything wrong or to deliberately hurt each other."

I drop my head on the chair back to look at the elaborate ceiling rose. I'm drained of energy, so I can only roll my eyes to the right to look at my husband—tall, erect, peering through the window onto the cobbled rear yard of the gallery.

"Will you ever be compelled to see her again?" I ask.

Can I even believe him however he may choose to answer?

"Never," he says without missing a beat.

I'm not quite as convinced as I was about mother's denial of having an affair with my uncle, but it's all Lawrence has to offer me in the here and now.

In truth, it's all anyone could possibly offer when the future is out of our hands.

Chapter 33
1931—Constance

"Finish your rice pudding, Dora," I say over my shoulder as I rush to answer the telephone.

The change in temperature in the hallway makes me wish already I was back in the cosy kitchen.

"Clayton 1625," I say, watching my daughter scrape the last of the jam from the bottom her bowl.

The pips travel down the line then, "Hello, Constance," is Gregory's chirpy greeting.

"Gregory, where are you calling from?"

"From home; I was just ringing to ask how you are."

"You mean, how my work is progressing. I hope you're not calling me to crack the whip," I say.

He chuckles and I imagine him in the hallway of the flat he has on Park Square in Leeds. I expect it will be the embodiment of a swanky bachelor pad.

"Hardly, but I hope your latest creation is coming along to replenish the vacant space on the gallery wall."

"Ah, I spotted that sale," I say. "I hope you got a fair price."

"Of course, I did. I'm an astute businessman who knows a good thing when he sees it. You're not a charity case, you know, Constance."

I worked on the painting he sold of our home sometimes in the dead of night when sleep was

266

elusive. The end result was a soulful almost ethereal vision of the cottage at dusk, one orange light glowing from the rear bedroom window. Gregory told me the dark atmosphere took the painting to another artistic level, enough to command a higher price.

Now I'm progressing nicely with my latest work, this time a lone dilapidated cottage on the moorland in springtime, one which I saw once on a walk with Lawrie when we first met. The countryside was an alien place to me then.

"Rest assured that you've earned your acclaim, Constance," Gregory says now. "Your work was always excellent, but now others appreciate it too; your painting wouldn't look out of place in the finest galleries of the capital. Truly, the Clarice Cliff of the canvas," he adds, tongue firmly in cheek and gently mocking. "

"Why thank you," I say, slightly embarrassed by the compliment though it warms the cockles of my heart. "It's rather a good job I have no intention of being poached from under your nose by another dealer, Gregory. I would never have sold a single painting if it wasn't for your eye."

A slight pause lengthens, so I realise the tide is set to turn in our conversation.

"Have you spoken to Lawrie since you last met in the gallery," he asks, trying and failing to have an air of nonchalance about his tone.

I blow out some air silently, noticing my pink cheeks in the hall mirror.

"We've only exchanged pleasantries when he's collected Dora to take her out for tea."

"Feel free to tell me to mind my own business, but how long do you think you can keep the status quo, my dear? Lawrie can't possibly continue living in a hotel room forever. It's such an awfully dreary place," he adds wryly, softening the harsh truth of his message.

"Mind your own business," I say kindly. "I've been thinking the same, of course. You might not believe me, but it just so happens I was going to telephone him this weekend to arrange to meet again."

"To tell him what?"

"Mr Coleman, you shall not coax my intentions from me before my husband has been made aware of them. Really, liberties are being taken."

I wonder now if he's fishing for information to pass on to Lawrence.

"Well, that's extremely dull of you if you don't mind me saying so. I shall hang up now if you have no gossip to offer me. Good day to you, Mrs Armitage."

"Good day, and rest assured that vacant spot on the wall of your gallery shall be filled within the week."

As I replace the telephone receiver, I catch sight of myself, a smile still hovering about my lips. I've never been one to look in the mirror constantly, a casual glance has always been sufficient.

Who is this woman staring back at me? Her hair is shining, her cheeks are aglow, all tension removed from the outline of her face if only for a moment.

Now though, my expression darkens when faced with reality.

I return to Dora who has decamped to the sitting room. She's ensconced in her father's chair, legs dangling, her forefinger tracing the line of words as she reads aloud quietly.

Child Whispers is a current favourite for both of us, giving Dora a first introduction to poetry. Her dark hair falling in waves either side of her face is the exact same shade of her father's. This weekend I will speak to Lawrie come what may.

I hover for a moment in the doorway watching her tiny mouth forming each syllable with care. She looks up from the page eventually to catch me soaking up the cosy little scene.

"Mummy, can we ..."

Her request is lost in the sound of the front door knocker. Saturdays usually find us alone as Mrs Osmond only works weekdays. I'm unable now to recall the last time we had visitors.

"Just a moment, sweetheart," I say as I retrace my steps to the door, spotting who our unexpected guest is through the glass panel.

"Gregory!" I exclaim, perplexed. "How in heaven's name did you get here so quickly?" I knew even as I was saying the words that it was impossible.

His eyes drop to his feet and my ears pound with a sense of alarm. Please don't say he's changed his mind about us; on reflection, I'm very clear about my misplaced feelings. He was the one who reminded me.

"I'm sorry my dear but a little subterfuge on my part. I was actually calling from the telephone box in the village. I'm afraid I have an ulterior motive."

My legs feel as though they might buckle, and I hold tightly onto the door handle for support.

He steps to one side, and I see a familiar car at the end of the drive.

"Lawrie," I whisper, his hesitant smile greeting me through the open window of the car. He looks nervous, like the night he proposed.

I look back at Gregory, my face a picture I can only imagine.

"Constance," he whispers, "this is not part of the plan, but please may I have a second or two of your time before I honour Lawrence's request."

I have no clue what is going on, but step to one side, narrowing the gap of the door without closing it, not wanting to shut Lawrence out completely.

"What is it, Gregory? You're worrying me now."

His complexion is grey and insipid, only increasing my concern.

"I've come to tell you that I'm going away for a while. To London in fact," he says. "Lawrence doesn't know though I expect you will tell him. Don't worry, our business arrangement shall continue of course, that goes without saying."

I stare at my friend, then shrug my shoulders, unable to find a suitable response. Moments ago, our telephone conversation gave no indication of this.

"I've arranged for an associate to run the gallery in my absence, and he will of course continue to sell your paintings."

"This is not what concerns me, Gregory. Why must you leave and so out of the blue… and without saying goodbye to Lawrence?"

He swallows as my eyes search his face.

"This isn't out of the blue for me, I've been thinking of taking a break for a while," he pauses, his cheeks turning puce, so they stand out from his pale face like a painted clown, "and I miss the bright lights darling," he adds in a mock jovial tone I see straight through. "The truth is I have a confession to make, Constance, and I'm afraid it will come as quite a shock."

Oh dear, it seems he really does have feelings for me after all. My stomach lurches.

"There's no artful way to say this to you, so I'll just have to get on with it. I was the one who reported your friend, Jennifer Pritchard, to the Board for passing off *Lewis's* designs. We were losing a lot of money from it, and I simply couldn't let it go unchallenged. Always the hard-nosed businessman, I'm afraid."

I can only stare at him in the stillness of the hallway. When the silence grows too uncomfortable, I hear his voice again.

"I suppose I had a bit of a crisis of conscience when I discovered Daphne Farrington was shouldering the blame. You must know that it was never my intention to hurt your feelings, but I just had to tell you before I left for London."

I fall against the wall, the mirror shifting to one side as I do and startling me.

"You; why would you do such a thing, Gregory? My ... our closest friend."

He's unable to bring himself to look at me.

"I know, I'm ashamed of my actions and you will understand now why I must go away." He holds a hand to his mouth. "Constance, believe me, I'm so terribly sorry. If it's any consolation, I was the one who persuaded them not to take the matter further."

My laugh is hollow.

"No Gregory, this is no consolation whatsoever, but why, why must you tell me now?"

"For many reasons: I came to realise I am ... was... in the middle of your relationship; my guilty conscience; the distress I've caused. I could go on, but what would it change? Lawrence is waiting. I just hope that someday you will find it within yourself to forgive me for being so devious."

Right now, it's impossible for me to think of someday when my husband is waiting to speak to me. This man confessing his wrongdoings in front of me does not deserve any more of my time.

"Yes, Lawrence is waiting. You should leave now, Gregory," I say quietly.

He runs a hand through his hair as I look upon a stranger in my home.

"Of course, but before I go, I must accomplish the mission I was set. The reason I am here is that Lawrence has asked me to inform you he would be delighted if you might consider accompanying him to the *Regal* picture house in Hunslet. There's a new musical film playing, the *City of Song*, which he thinks you might enjoy."

A trip to a Saturday matinee at the picture house of my childhood hometown is the most wonderful gesture on my husband's part, yet all I can think of is banishing this man from my home.

"Mrs Osmond is on standby to look after Dora, if you would honour him with your presence this afternoon," he says.

I think of Dora in the sitting room by the fireside, settled for an afternoon at home with her mother. I think of her father sitting in the car, filled with apprehension, the future of our marriage out of his control. My palm covers my mouth as I gasp, and Gregory puts his hand on my arm.

"I'm sorry Constance but I owed it to you to tell you the truth in person before I left."

I shake his hand free, wiping a tear with my forefinger. Clearing my throat, I stand as tall as my back will stretch.

"Mr Coleman, I would be grateful if you could thank my husband for his request ... but I think an afternoon at home in the bosom of his loving family might be more fulfilling for all parties concerned."

Gregory stares at me a moment before bowing slightly and walking out of the door.

I gather my emotions and try to line them up before I can reconcile with my husband, giving our reunion the attention it deserves. Gregory Coleman's confession can wait for the time being. It must wait.

I watch Gregory now as he leans into the passenger seat window of the car to speak to Lawrie. Hardly a moment passes before Lawrie leaves the car and slams the door.

Timothy waves before driving away and I manage to return his wave although my world has almost ground to a halt. I lean against the doorframe as Lawrie waits at the gate, our eyes never straying from each other. They never stray all the while he walks up the pathway, while he steps over the threshold and stands looking down at me only inches away. The hollows of his eyes are a reminder of the pain he has endured; now I must take that pain away.

I want to take that pain away.

My hand goes to the sleeve of his coat without thinking, pulling him down towards me to bring about a clash of our lips so we kiss as though we have never kissed before.

My husband has come home to me, and he is where he should be. This is the only place he will ever belong.

His arms tighten around me when we eventually pull away from our kiss and I press my cheek to his coat, the outside air still clinging to the woollen fabric.

I peer through the panel of glass once more and see Gregory's car driving past the house. He must have parked near the green to take so long to reach here. I notice he too has a rear passenger though they are looking straight ahead so I'm unable to see who it is. Perhaps a client, perhaps his latest muse, I really couldn't care less in this moment.

Just before the car disappears, the passenger seems unable to stop themselves turning their face towards the front door of our cottage.

It was the briefest of glances, but I now know who was hiding in wait for Gregory to return from his mission.

I close my eyes and bury my face into my husband's chest. We have said so much without words just like the Constance and Lawrence of old.

"Daddy, it's you!" Dora shrieks, "I thought it was Uncle Gregory."

We pull apart, but Lawrie's arm remains a comforting blanket around my shoulders until he bends to greet our daughter.

The afternoon stretches ahead for us, and I intend to languish in our little family.

As for Daphne Farrington, she may have a plan in mind. Perhaps she sees Gregory as a step toward a brand, spanking new future for herself and her child or they may be madly in love for all I know.

As for Gregory, his personal life has always been something of a closed book, even to us who were supposedly his closest friends. But seeing him with her I think how ironic that the man who outwardly extols perfection should be taken by a woman on the rebound.

Gregory is free to come and go as he chooses, and if she breaks his heart, then on his own head it shall be. He must be aware of where her heart lies, or perhaps she's managed to convince him otherwise.

After a moment of listening to Dora chattering to her father, the three of us head into the sitting room. As I close the door to our little world behind us however, a sensation wafts over me like a sweet, calming breeze.

For the last twelve years I've been on full alert, drowning in a sense of foreboding that filled me at times with crippling anxiety.

That woman has gone.

Now, I finally know what I feel towards the woman who is and probably will be in love with my husband for the rest of her life.

Nothing … absolutely nothing.

About the author

Jo Priestley is a Yorkshire author committed to writing historical fiction, based on real lives and real people. She grew up with tales by the fireside, poignantly told by her grandmother, in her crumbling but grand house on the outskirts of Leeds, England, creating the perfect atmosphere.

She has been a professional business writer all her career, and now she would like to share the fictional stories that have been waiting in the wings, until the time was right.

After almost ten years of writing, six novels were published in 2023, with her next book due to be published in June 2024. The books feature women who have their own tale of love, life and friendship to tell, and are set in and around Bronte Country. She is a proud member of the Society of Authors.

Jo considers the raising of five strong, kind-hearted daughters to adulthood her greatest achievement. Now she would like to commit herself as much to her passion for storytelling.

Printed in Great Britain
by Amazon